By Lynne Sella

THE DEPUTY SARAH MURDOCK SERIES
Grave Robber
Snake Charmer
Horse Wrangler

BETWEEN THE CRIMES BOOKS
A Picture Perfect Romance

HORSE WRANGLER

Lynne Sella

WingSpan Press

Published in the United States and the United Kingdom by WingSpan Press, Livermore, CA

The WingSpan name, logo and colophon are the trademarks of WingSpan Publishing.

ISBN 978-1-59594-637-9 (pbk.)
ISBN 978-1-59594-953-0 (ebk.)

First edition 2019

Printed in the United States of America

www.wingspanpress.com

Library of Congress Control Number 2019937000

1 2 3 4 5 6 7 8 9 10

This book is dedicated to Zellamae Miles, a longtime friend of the family, fellow book club member, and one of my biggest fans. Though she is gone, memories of her remain.

Acknowledgements

Several years ago, we accepted an invitation to visit friends who had recently moved to Modoc County. Dropping down into Surprise Valley during that first visit, I realized I had found the setting for my novel, and the idea for the Deputy Sarah Murdock series was born. Therefore, I would like to thank Mike and Lindee Larsen, whose exploration and knowledge of this unique place and interesting locations in the surrounding area have been invaluable. A special thanks to Nick Retterath for sharing his years of experience with wild horse round-ups, Dusty Vaughn for imparting his vast knowledge and expertise of the art of barbecue, and Chip Jackson for answering my numerous questions about the world of law enforcement. And finally, I am grateful to Rosalee Bradley and Ginger Bill for sharing their adventures as well as their love of endurance riding.

Horse Wrangler

Chapter 1

"Unit 113, Modoc County."

"Go ahead Modoc, this is 113."

"Sarah! There's a report of a 10-32 at the Thomson place at the end of County Road 14. I've already dispatched the ambulance."

"Copy. I just passed that location. ETA is five minutes."

"Copy, 113. Time is 16:20."

Reaching the ninety degree turn on County Road 1 just east of Lake City, I flew off the pavement onto a small dirt road that reconnected with the asphalt on the other side and headed back the way I had come. I flipped down my visor and scanned the list of codes. Having been a deputy sheriff in Modoc County for about nine months, I was familiar with most of them, but this one didn't ring a bell. *Drowning!* No wonder the dispatcher, Cindy Evans, sounded upset. Unseasonably hot weather was probably to blame; I just hoped I'd get there in time.

I turned left onto County Road 14, and the back of the Explorer fishtailed as the tires momentarily lost traction. Not seeing anyone in front of the house when I reached the end of the road, I followed the driveway around to the left and spotted a white-haired man standing on the edge of a small pond about a hundred yards away. Leaning on a cane and throwing some kind of rope toward the center of the pond, he turned when I skidded to a stop not far from him.

"Here! Over here!" he cried, waving his cane at me.

Barely taking time to throw the transmission in park and turn off the engine, I leapt from my vehicle and ran toward him.

"In there!" he hollered, motioning toward the pond.

I spotted the victim, wearing jeans and a blue hoodie, facedown on the surface of the water. "How deep?" I yelled, stopping just long enough to unholster my gun and drop it on the ground along with my cell phone.

"Chest high I 'spect," he replied, indicating the depth on his own body.

I jumped in, scissor kicking my legs to keep my head above the surface. As soon as my toes came in contact with the spongy bottom, I moved toward the victim. My heart raced as I pushed and pulled myself through water that practically covered my shoulders. With no detectable movement, the arms and legs seemed strangely stiff. Finally, I got close enough to throw my arm around the victim's waist and immediately realized something was horribly wrong. Rolling the body over, I found myself staring into the lifeless eyes of a mannequin.

"They okay?" the old man called from the bank, squinting in the bright sun to get a better look.

"We're good," I panted, making my way back to the edge of the pond and pulling the mannequin along behind me. When I got close enough, I heaved it out of the water and scrambled up the slick bank.

"Why, it's a dummy!" he said, poking at it with his cane. His eyes narrowed, and his face turned a dark red.

I pushed my sunglasses onto the top of my head. "I think someone has played a joke on you—a very cruel joke," I said, untucking my uniform shirt and squeezing water out of it. Although my sudden dip in the pond had cooled me off, being drenched was most unpleasant.

"A joke? This here ain't funny! I 'bout had myself a heart attack when I saw that in the water!" He jabbed the mannequin again with his cane.

"I'm sure you did. And no, it's not funny." I poked my shirt back into my waistband as best as I could. Retrieving my gun and cell phone, I heard a faint giggle coming from a nearby shed. "Do you live here alone, Mr. Thomson?"

"No, it's me and the missus, but she's gone to town to get a few groceries."

"I see." I pulled my notebook out of my back pocket but quickly realized it was useless as it was soaking wet, and its pages were stuck together. "If you'll just step over to my patrol unit with me, I'll take down your name and contact information."

"You betcha," he said and followed along behind me.

I reached up and keyed my mike. "Modoc, Unit..." I began and then stopped when I suddenly remembered my radio had taken the plunge with me. Fairly certain the water had damaged it, I opened my door and grabbed the mic inside. "Modoc, Unit 113."

"Go ahead, 113."

"I'm Code 4, and you can cancel the ambulance. It's a false alarm."

"Thank goodness! I mean, copy 113. Time is 16:38."

I replaced the mic just as the rancher got to my rig. "Mr. Thomson—"

"Name's Tom," he interrupted, "but you can call me TJ."

"Okay, TJ." I lowered my voice and leaned closer. "I think whoever did this is still on your property."

"That so?" He looked around. "Whereabouts?"

I gestured toward the small shed. "In there."

"Well, what are we waitin' for? Let's go roust 'em outta there right now!" The old man made a little hop on his good leg and pivoted to the right until he was facing the shed. "I'll teach 'em to play a trick on me!"

"Now hold on a second," I said, resting my hand on his arm. "We don't know who's in there, but I'd be willing to bet it's just kids." Noticing the beads of sweat covering his face, I dropped my sunglasses into place and said, "Why don't you go sit in the shade on your back porch, and I'll go get whoever is in the shed and bring them over."

He stared at me for several seconds and finally let out a huge sigh. "All right," he said and started for the house.

As I approached the small outbuilding, I noticed the side facing the pond had a hole the size of a brick about three feet up from the ground. *A good spot to watch the action.* Scuffling sounds came from inside, and just as I was about to reach for the door, it burst open and two very sweaty, tousle-haired boys darted past me, one on each side. I quickly spun around and was able to snag the collar of each damp T-shirt before they got too far. "Whoa, there fellas! What's the hurry?"

"Hey, let go! We didn't do nothing!" the taller of the two exclaimed.

4

"Is that so?" I said as I guided them toward the back of TJ's house. "Looks like trespassing to me. I doubt Mr. Thomson gave you permission to hang out in his shed. What's your name?" I shook the taller boy's shirt so he'd know I was addressing him.

For a few steps, there was no reply. Finally, he answered. "Frank. And his name is Ramona," he added, pointing to his co-conspirator.

"Shut-up Francis, my name's Ray and you know it!"

I pulled their collars a little higher. "That's enough, you two. March."

As we rounded the large lilac bush at the end of the crumbling sidewalk, TJ burst out of his chair. "You!" he exclaimed, shaking his cane in our direction. "I should've known you'd pull a stunt like this."

"You know these boys?" I asked.

"Sure do." He aimed his cane at Frank as if it were a sword. "This here scallywag lives on Road 15, directly south of the field in front of my place and runs around with that hoodlum," he said, swinging his cane toward the other boy. "I've run them off of here more times than I care to remember. Keep catching them in my pond."

"We ain't hurting nothing." Ray folded his skinny arms across his slight chest. "Just trying to cool off is all."

"That old pond's dangerous," TJ said, shaking his head. "I told them someone could..." He paused for a moment and then glared at the boys. "Drown!"

Frank and Ray glanced at each other and snickered.

"I don't think you two realize the seriousness of this situation," I said, resting one hand on my gun belt and the other one on the butt of my Sig 9mm. "Besides trespassing, your actions perpetrated a hoax that resulted in a 911 call, which ended in a false alarm—not to mention scaring Mr. Thomson here half to death." I crossed my arms and gave the boys my best deputy glare. Of course, I was bluffing. With no damage to personal property, the most they were guilty of was trespassing. However, they didn't know that, and my plan seemed to be working. The smiles vanished from their faces, and their eyes darted between me, the ground, and each other.

"What they need is a trip to the woodshed!" TJ exclaimed, jabbing the end of his cane into the dirt.

"Well, that'll be up to their parents." I retrieved my cell phone from my pocket. "Who wants to go first?"

The boys looked at each other, and the color visibly drained from their faces. "It was his idea," Frank mumbled, staring at his feet and motioning toward his friend with his elbow.

"Shut up, Francis!"

"Well, it was!"

"But my folks ain't home!" Ray blurted.

"Who are you staying with?" I asked.

"My uncle up in Bidwell."

"Well, you can call him then."

"But..."

"But what?"

Ray glanced at Frank before answering. "He thinks...I mean, I told him..." He looked at Frank again.

"Ray got the dummy from his uncle," Frank said.

"He what?" TJ exclaimed.

"Did he know what you were going to do with it?" I asked.

Ray shook his head. "I told him me and Frank were gonna make a scarecrow."

"Well, it sure enough scared me," TJ said, dropping back into his chair.

One at a time, each boy made a phone call and explained what he had done before handing the phone over to me. I informed each adult I spoke to that there would be no formal charges this time but if caught at the Thomson place again, they would be transported to the Sheriff's Office. Then I had the two boys haul the mannequin to my patrol unit and get in the backseat.

"If they show up again, don't confront them, just give me a call," I told TJ as I handed him one of my cards out of the center console since the ones in my shirt pocket were soggy, "and I'll come pick them up."

"Will do," he said and moseyed back toward the house.

It was a very quiet trip as I delivered each boy to his place of residence. A few minutes later, I had retrieved my dog from my full-time neighbor and part-time partner, Remy Hamilton, and headed home. Too hot for a soak in my custom hot tub, I settled for an ice-cold beer beside the small creek that runs through my property just northwest of Fort Bidwell. Dangling my feet in the cold water and watching my dust mop of a dog explore nearby, I cleared my mind of the eventful afternoon, grateful it was only a prank. *What a way to end the week!*

Chapter 2

The young horse swung its head around and almost knocked Scott off his feet. "Dammit, don't let him do that!" He repositioned the horse's hoof on his left knee and continued prying the compacted dirt out of it with a hoof pick.

"Sorry," I said, getting a better grip on the Arabian's lead rope. "It's not as easy as you think."

"Holding a horse?"

I rolled my eyes. "No, we're talking about competing in an endurance ride, remember?"

"Oh, that. How hard can it be? It's just a timed trail ride." Scott Jenkins flashed his crooked smile at me as he released the horse's hoof and straightened up. Not only was he a fellow deputy sheriff, we'd gone to high school together and competed on the rodeo circuit during our senior year. And after I'd lived on the east coast for nearly eight years as an FBI agent, it was great to rekindle our friendship as well as our shared love of horses.

"There's a lot more to it than that," I insisted. "One mistake can cost you more than just the race."

"Don't you think that's exaggerating it a little," he said as he moved toward the back of the horse and reached for a rear hoof. Without warning, the horse kicked out with it and then came within inches of stepping on Scott's left foot. "Stop that, Raz!" he scolded, smacking the horse on the rump. Before it could retaliate, he shoved the horse over with his shoulder and snatched up the hind foot.

"By the way, I've been meaning to ask you how you came up with that name."

"His registered name is RazzleDazzle," Scott answered between grunts as he and the horse fought for control of the foot. "Most of the time, though, he's more of a spaz."

I laughed. "Why's that?"

Scott finished cleaning Raz's hoof and released it, stepping well away to avoid any more of the horse's shenanigans. "Well, you've seen how he acts sometimes when we're working with him—focused and listening one minute and a complete idiot afraid of his own shadow the next."

Reminds me of an old high school chum I work with!

He led the horse a few feet away and pulled off his halter. "Maybe I should enter him in one of those competitions," Scott said, watching the Arabian kick up his hind feet and fart across the field. "That might mellow him out."

"I'm not so sure..." I stopped. Originally, I'd planned on asking Scott to be my support crew. But maybe having him on the ride would be more fun, and then he would see firsthand how challenging it can be. "On second thought, why not. But you'll have to start training right away. The race is less than a month away, but there's still time to enter."

"Training? For what?"

"It's more grueling than you think. You and your

horse need to be as physically fit as possible to pass the vet checks during the race."

"Well, Raz is young and runs all over this pasture every day. And I'm as fit as I was in high school," Scott said, standing very tall and throwing out his chest. I didn't have the heart to tell him it no longer stuck out past the small potbelly he had developed over the last few years. Most likely a side effect of all the Pink Snowballs he'd eaten out of the vending machine in the break room at work.

"It's still a good idea to work with your horse, practice traveling over different types of terrain at different paces—on the horse and off. And there could be tricky water crossings or narrow bridges with no railings. I've been riding Raven up around Fee Reservoir." I'd purchased my Thoroughbred gelding when I lived on the east coast, and we were always competing. However, since moving back to California, we hadn't spent much time pleasure riding let alone competing. "But I'm thinking about going farther into the Hays Canyon Range. The terrain looks very similar to the area where the Red Rock Rumble takes place."

"Red Rock Rumble? Still sounds like the trail ride competitions me and Fancy used to go on," he said, picking up the grooming tools and tossing them back into the five-gallon bucket he kept them in.

"Yeah, but that Arabian of yours is not surefooted, reliable Fancy—you just said so yourself." I followed him into the small metal shed he used as a tack room. "It's taken this long to get Raz somewhat manageable." I'd been helping Scott work with that horse since I moved back and taken a job as deputy sheriff. We'd made lots of progress, but the horse was still unpredictable—the complete opposite of the horse he'd had in high school. And even Fancy had had her moments.

"Okay, so maybe he could use a little more work out on the open range but..." A loud crash coming from one of the back corners of the shed interrupted him. "What the heck was that?" He moved toward the sound, but before he got very close, a small, dusty white dog with matted fur popped out from behind the large feed can. "Dog, what are you doing back there?"

"Come here Bubbles," I said, snatching up my tiny mutt.

"Don't you ever give that thing a bath?" Scott hung up the halter and the lead rope. "And what kind of name is Bubbles?"

"I told you—that's what Alexis named him."

"Who?"

"Alexis...oh sorry. Lydia." My sister, who had been named after my grandmother on my father's side of the family, changed her name when she was hired on at Nordstrom. She felt Alexis was more sophisticated; my father disagreed. "Remy calls him Bubba."

"Now that name fits him way better."

"I know. I just haven't gotten into the habit yet, I guess. So, are you serious about entering the race?" I asked as we exited the shed, and I set Bubbles back on the ground.

"Yeah, why not."

"Okay then, I'll email you the link to the website so you can register, but the deadline is soon."

"Okay, sure. That'll work." We strolled toward my Ford Dooley.

"And you really should think about training," I repeated.

"All right, all right." He turned and headed for the doublewide modular sitting on the three acres of pasture that he rents for next to nothing. "See you at work," he called over his shoulder.

I pulled open my truck door and waited for Bubbles to get a running start before leaping up into my seat and over the center console into his favorite spot. I climbed in after him, fired up the diesel engine, and followed the short dirt road back to Highway 299 just west of Alturas. As I began the climb into the Warner Mountains headed for Cedar Pass, I realized I still needed a support crew, and by the time I pulled into Cedarville, I knew exactly who I was going to ask.

The crowd at the Silver Spur Saloon on a Saturday afternoon typically consists of a handful of regulars. The quiet atmosphere and cool interior always seems so inviting, especially with the weather being so hot lately, and I was surprised it hadn't attracted more patrons. A small television nestled among the liquor bottles under the grimy mirror was tuned to the NASCAR race and had the full attention of owner/bartender, Pete Yarbrough. Dressed in his typical black jeans and two-toned bowling shirt, he leaned with his back against the bar.

Using my best stealth skills, I approached the barstool directly behind him and climbed aboard. It wasn't until a commercial caused a break in the action that he turned around and noticed me.

"Sarah! Long time no see."

"Yeah, I know. Sorry." I leaned forward and rested

my forearms on the polished surface of the bar. "I've been spending every spare moment I've had training with Raven."

"Training, huh? For what?"

"Well, after hauling you and your motorcycle to the race in the desert, I realized how much I missed competing myself. So I signed up for an endurance ride."

"Good for you. Buy you a beer?"

"Sure, give me a Miller."

"High Life or MGD?"

"Hmm, how about a MGD."

"Coming right up." Pete reached into the small refrigerated unit below the television, pulled out a clear bottle with a black label and popped the top on it as he sat it in front of me. "Now, tell me more about this competition."

As I sipped my ice-cold beer, I explained—for a second time that day—the basics of an endurance ride. "I signed up for the shorter race, of course, just thirty miles, but now that Scott is going to compete with me, I have to find someone else to be our support crew."

Pete poured himself a cup of thick, dark liquid from the Mr. Coffee that sat next to the electronic cash register and leaned against the shelf, facing me. "So just what exactly does a support crew do?" he asked, tucking his left hand into his right armpit and sipping the hot beverage from a small, brown ceramic mug.

"Well, not much really. The person has to make sure there's hay and buckets for water in the hold area, have replacement bottles of water for my saddlebags as well as extra snacks for the riders and horses. Then after we head back out on the trail, get things ready for the end of the race."

"Seems easy enough. Where's the race?"

Before I could answer, a customer at the other end of the bar got Pete's attention. He set down his mug and covered the distance in three easy strides.

"Nevada," I said when he returned. "Somewhere off Red Rock Road north of Reno. I printed off the directions and it's supposed to be marked with ribbons."

He nodded. "And when?"

"Just a few weeks or so from now. That's why I've been working with Raven. We both have gotten a little out of shape since I moved back."

"Oh, I think your shape is just fine," Pete said, winking one of his crystal-blue eyes at me.

Oh brother! We had grown closer over the past few months. Sharing a traumatic event, being rescued, the exchange of a kiss or two not to mention, well...you know...can take a friendship to the next level. And while we weren't in a hot and heavy relationship, we were definitely good friends who enjoyed each other's company. "Oh knock it off," I scolded. "You know as well as I do, the more physically fit you are, the better you can compete."

His eyes twinkled as a huge grin spread from his black mustache to his Elvis style sideburns. "Of course I do, but that was just too good to pass up."

"So, what do you say?" I asked, ignoring his comment. "Will you be our support crew?"

"No problemo," he replied. "Besides I owe you one, remember?"

I flashed on his motorcycle race in the desert and

quickly hoped that my competition would be way less complicated. "Great! We can work out the logistics in the next week or two."

"Sounds like a plan—and speaking of plans," he said, taking my empty and wiping the bar where it had been. "Whatd'ya say to getting together tomorrow? That is, if you can fit me into your schedule."

"Well, Sundays have been my longer training sessions. I've been thinking about going into the Hays Canyon Range at the end of dirt 299. The trails and terrain seem comparable to what we'll find at the competition. But with this heat, I'll be getting as early a start as I can, so I should be done by noon."

"Great. My dad sent me a new dry rub to try, so how about if I call Shellie and you talk to Remy about getting together at my place?"

So much for it being just the two of us!

"Okay. What can we bring?"

Pete chuckled. "You can bring beer and tell Remy he can bring whatever he wants."

I glared at Pete. I wasn't a great cook; I wasn't even a good cook, but there were a few things I could make that were edible—most of the time. *And it certainly is way better than my sister's cooking!* "Fine. I'll bring the beer," I said, sliding off my barstool and starting for the door. "See you tomorrow."

Chapter 3

The third time I hit the snooze button, I had serious doubts about my decision, but it had to be done; Raven and I needed to step-up our training. As I threw back the covers and swung my feet out of bed, the small fur ball curled up on the foot of my bed whimpered in protest. "At least you get to stay at Remy's and play with Millie, while Raven and I go running around in this heat."

Millie was a small white goat I had sort of rescued—or stolen—depending on whose point of view was being given. Figuring I couldn't care for the animal properly, Remy had adopted it and promptly named it Millie, after his white-haired grandmother.

I trudged into the bathroom, splashed water on my face and quickly braided my hair into a single braid down my back. Then I exchanged my oversized Green Bay Packers shirt I wore as a nightgown for a pair of cutoff sweats and a loose-fitting T-shirt. Donning a pair of socks and my cross-trainers, I was ready to load up Raven.

As I left the bedroom, I plucked the fur ball off my bed and set him on the floor. "Come on, Bubbles. Time to get going." The small dog shook his body and pattered after me into the kitchen, where I tossed an apple, a few bottles of water, a couple packets of trail mix and a protein bar (having traded them for my Pop-Tarts while training) into a plastic grocery bag. Grabbing my keys, wallet, and sunglasses as I passed through the sunroom that doubled as my office, I locked the front door behind us and headed for the barn. Passing my Ford Dooley, I scooped up the tiny mutt and tossed him and the bag of snacks inside, glad I'd installed motion-activated spotlights on the bathhouse and barn a few weeks ago. They allowed me to navigate the long driveway and occasionally spot Raven as he moved close to the beam of light.

Knowing how difficult it can be to hook up to a horse trailer by myself in the dark, I'd taken care of that the day before and packed up my gear as well. All I had to do was catch Raven and load him into the trailer, which isn't as easy as it sounds when it's dark and the horse is black. Using a can of oats I'd retrieved from the tack room, I was able to lure in the large horse, and he was haltered and loaded in just a few minutes.

A quick stop at Remy's to drop off Bubbles, and we were on the way to Cedarville, the thirty minute drive giving both of us plenty of time to munch on a small breakfast before training. Five miles from the end of the pavement on 299 and just inside the Nevada border, I found a nice wide spot in the road to pull over. By the time I had my horse unloaded, the pale light of predawn had appeared.

As I carefully saddled Raven, I could feel his anticipation building under my touch, each adjustment causing him to shift his weight from one side to the other and occasionally paw at the dirt with a hoof. "Easy, Boy." I rubbed his massive neck. "We have a lot of work ahead of us." With everything in place, I looped the reins over his head and took ahold of the lead rope attached to the ring on the underside of the combination halter and bridle headstall I used. After one last check to make sure the saddlebags were secure, we began our workout by walking at a brisk pace through the large sagebrush.

Ten minutes later we were comfortably jogging along, weaving around the vegetation. When we reached the first drop in the terrain, I decided we were sufficiently warmed up, and it was time to get into the saddle. I slipped my foot into the stirrup until it touched the heavy leather guard, which prevented my foot from sliding through, swung my other leg over, and we were off.

Traveling up and down hills, on trails or cross-country, we navigated back and forth along the Hays Canyon Range, dodging sagebrush and an occasional juniper tree. We alternated between gaits until, four hours and three water bottles later, we arrived at the top of a hill about a quarter of a mile from the truck. The steep incline, dotted with juniper trees and rock outcroppings, was perfect to end our training session. I dismounted, threw the reins over Raven's neck again, and we began our descent.

Our paces were perfectly matched as we negotiated a path around the largest outcropping about two-thirds of the way down the hill. We'd almost reached the bottom when I heard a strange pounding sound getting louder and louder. I turned around just in time to see a band of horses come barreling over the top of the hill and head straight for us. Raven exploded, pulling on the lead rope so hard it pulled me off my feet and tore the rope from my hands. And then he was gone, running balls out toward the road.

Glancing back up the hill, the only thing I saw were horses swerving around trees and leaping down off the rock outcroppings. I had to get out of the way. As quickly as I could, I crawled over to the nearest juniper tree, pulled myself to my feet, and forced my body amongst its branches, ignoring their poking and scratching. I held my breath as the large animals rushed by me, often passing within a foot of where I was hiding as they brushed by the tree.

A full minute ticked by after the last animal had run past me before I stepped clear of my refuge. As I straightened my sunglasses and began taking inventory of the cuts and bruises that covered my arms and legs, a small yellow helicopter burst over the top of the hill, its skids just barely skimming over the tops of the trees. That's when I realized Raven and I had been caught in a wild horse roundup. I ran toward my truck, but the moment my foot hit the dirt road I knew I was in trouble. With no pockets, I had tucked the keys into my saddlebags where they would be safe—unless my horse ran off—which he did. I had no other choice but to head towards Cedarville and hope that somehow I would catch up with Raven eventually.

I broke into a jog, focusing on the rhythmic movement of my feet to keep from panicking. If I had to, I was sure I could reach Cedarville by mid-afternoon but finding Raven could prove to be more of a challenge. Entering the road on a decline, I moved at a fairly quick pace, but I had no idea how long I'd have to sustain it. I hadn't passed any signs of a roundup when I traveled the road several hours ago, so I had no idea how far the wild horses were being moved.

A sharp turn to the left, and the road straightened out into a flat sweeping turn heading west toward Surprise Valley. Without the benefit of downhill, my pace slowed slightly and my breathing became more labored. Feeling the sweat run down my back and wishing I had another sip of tepid water from one of the remaining bottles in my saddlebags, I watched my feet shoot out in front of me, one at a time. *Gotta keep going!* As I glanced up to see how far I'd traveled, I almost tripped when I saw something in the road about three hundred yards away, galloping toward me. *Raven!* But as I got closer, I realized it wasn't my runaway but a person dressed like a cowboy astride a large sorrel horse. *Saved!*

Stride by stride, we shortened the distance between us. "Am I glad to see you," I panted when we finally met.

"Howdy ma'am," the man said, touching the wide, flat brim of his cowboy hat. "You look like you could use a hand."

I nodded. "My ride spooked when the wild horses came over the hill and got away from me. Have you seen him?"

The man chuckled. "Yeah, we were sure surprised when he came in, leading the herd. We wondered where he'd come from 'til the helicopter pilot radioed in that there was someone on foot, so I hightailed it out here. Name's Nate." He leaned down and offered me his right hand.

"I'm Sarah," I replied, returning the gesture.

"Climb on up, and I'll take you down to the catchin'

pens. We don't wanna be here when the second group comes through, or we both might be walking." He slipped his well-worn boot out of the stirrup next to me and this time extended his left arm.

Standing next to the horse so I was facing Nate, I twisted the stirrup slightly so I could slide my left foot in, grasped the inside of his left elbow, and swung my leg over the sorrel's back. The moment I had my seat and a firm grip on the cantle of his western saddle, he spun the horse around and we quickly transitioned from walk to trot to an easy lope.

Minutes ticked by as I struggled to maintain my position. It's not easy riding behind a saddle, especially when traveling faster than a walk, and by the time the road made its final turn west and we'd reached the top of the hill that looked down into Surprise Valley, the muscles in my arms and legs ached. We slowed to a brisk walk, and I was amazed by what I saw. Temporary fencing formed a massive V, funneling the horses into a large oval-shaped holding pen constructed of portable panels. Connected to that were two smaller round pens, and wranglers—some on horseback and some on foot—were working on separating the captured animals. "When did all this get set-up?" I asked Nate.

"Oh, we rolled in about six-thirty and had this all in place in just under an hour."

"Wow, that's impressive."

"Well, we pretty much got it down to a system. We haul the panels in on that flat bed you see hooked to the semi. Most of us work on getting those in place, while the rest work on stringing the jute fence," he said, guiding his horse around the end of the temporary barrier and following it toward the pens. Just before we reached them, he veered off to the left and headed for a group of livestock trailers parked along the south side of the road. "You'll find your horse tied up on the backside of that white livestock trailer," he said, pulling his boot out of the left stirrup again and leaning forward and slightly to the right. "It's less stressful if the horses we aren't using can't see what's going on."

"Thanks for the ride." I dismounted and stretched my legs.

"Sure thing," he said and rode off.

I darted around the trailer and was relieved to see Raven standing there, securely tethered and munching on some hay. "There you are, you scoundrel." I scratched the white star on his massive forehead, and then quickly rubbed my hands down each leg and checked all four hooves. *No injuries, thank goodness!* After grabbing the last water bottle out of my saddlebags, I gave him a playful slap on the rump and wandered over to the catching pens to check out the action.

As I approached the largest of the three pens, I immediately recognized Lulu DeLoure, a reporter from the *Alturas Gazette.* Her short blond hair adorned with a shock of neon pink right above her forehead was unmistakable. She had exchanged her plaid skirt and frilly blouse she usually wore for a pair of fashion jeans and an orange short sleeve T-shirt that really clashed with her hair. Bonnie Patterson, a BLM biologist I'd met a few months ago, stood beside her. Deep in conversation, Lulu was hastily scribbling in a notebook; I assumed gathering information for her next newspaper article. Not too far away from them and definitely looking out of place, a man and two women were also talking as they watch the wranglers.

"Hello Bonnie," I said when I was close enough.

"Why hello, Deputy," Lulu said, cutting off Bonnie's opportunity to reply. "I didn't expect to see you out here."

I smiled. "I'm a little surprised to be here myself," I answered. "Are you working on your next big story?"

"Oh yes!" As she pushed the red frames of her oversized glasses back into position on the bridge of her nose, I wondered if she were colorblind. "Wild horse round-ups are quite controversial," she continued. "That's why they're here." She nodded at the trio and leaned closer. "Protestors," she whispered.

"Really?" I glanced at Bonnie, who smiled and shrugged her shoulders ever so slightly. "They seem kinda quiet for protestors, don't you think?"

Lulu paused for a few seconds. "You know, you're right. Time to ask them a few questions." She flipped her notebook closed, picked up the bag that had been on the ground near her feet, and strode over to the small group.

"Are you here in an official capacity?" I asked Bonnie as she and I leaned against the portable panel in front of us and watched the last of the wild horses ushered out of the large catching pen.

"Nope. I just came by to watch. What about you?" she asked.

"Purely accidental," I said and left it at that.

"Chopper says he's on the way back," someone yelled. "Let's get set up."

"Now you'll get to see firsthand how a roundup's done," said a voice behind us. I turned to find Nate, minus his mount, approaching us along with another wrangler who looked like he'd seen several roundups in his lifetime. "This second group won't be quite as large as the first one, but it will still be something to watch."

"I think one of the horses got out," I said, pointing toward the jute fence flanking the left side of the V.

"Nah, that's Old Red." Nate propped his right foot on one of the lower cross bars of the panel. "See the guy leading him?" I looked again and could just make out a pair of human legs on the far side of the animal as it moved along the fence. "He's gonna come around the end of the fence and come back along the inside about halfway and then wait."

"What for?" I asked.

"Old Red is a prada horse. He'll get released when the herd gets closer and lead them right into the catching pen."

"Judas horse," Nate's companion said.

"What?" I peered at him over my shoulder.

"He's a Judas horse not a prada horse."

"What's the difference?"

"Ain't none." Nate said. "There's just some—" He nodded at the other wrangler. "—that think the prada horse is more of a traitor to its kind, so they call it a Judas horse."

"Just makes more sense," his friend said, folding his arms across his chest. "And it don't sound prissy like prada does." Bonnie and I glanced at each other and smiled.

As we scanned the horizon for signs of the approaching herd, a light-colored car pulled up behind us. Nate did a double take. "Sonofabitch! Should've figured it was too good to be true."

"Who's that?" I asked.

"That there is the biggest pain in the... "

"Here they come," someone shouted before Nate had a chance to finish.

"You'll see soon enough. Come on Earl," he said, addressing his companion, "time to go to work." As soon as the two men walked away, things began to happen very quickly.

Chapter 4

A small herd of wild horses appeared at the top of the hill, traveling at an easy lope. In less than a minute, they had covered half of the distance to the catching pen.

"Oh look," I said, pointing to the jute fence on the left, "they've released the... "

"LET THEM GO!" an amplified voice blasted behind us, causing Bonnie and me to jump. The voice came from a rather small woman who quickly approached the other protestors standing near the large catching pen. Instead of packing a typical cone-shaped megaphone, I was surprised to see she was wearing a handsfree headset connected to something resembling a small Bose radio that she had attached at her waist. "LET THEM GO!" The horses closest to her spooked and spun back toward the entrance they'd just passed through, causing the wranglers to scramble in order to keep them under control. Using the camera she wore around her neck, she began snapping pictures before booming out another "LET THEM GO!"

As the other protestors moved away, I spotted Nate rushing across the pen and heading straight for her. Although I couldn't make out what he was saying, his wildly waving arms were a clear indicator he was not happy.

"These people are from the Cloud Foundation," Lulu said, having led the trio over to us. "They go to wild horse roundups to document how the animals are treated."

"So what's with her?" Bonnie asked.

The taller woman shook her head. "I truly have no idea. Carol Ganns," she said, offering her hand to each of us. "This is Alan Parker and Veronica Pitman."

"Ronnie to my friends," the shorter woman shared, placing her hand on her chest and smiling.

"Is she part of your group?" I asked, watching the boisterous protestor make her way around to the second, smaller pen.

"Absolutely not! I don't know how, but she just shows up, often creating more of a problem. Are you getting this, Alan?" Carol asked.

"On it," he replied, starting the small video recorder he'd been holding. "Rolling."

"We've all tried to reason with her," Ronnie added, "but she won't listen to any of us."

"From what I've seen, I thought this roundup was going well," Bonnie said.

Carol nodded. "Oh, I agree. The helicopter never seemed to get too close, allowing the horses to travel at a slower pace. The catching pen is larger, so they calmed down a bit before the separating started. And see how the connecting chutes are at least three panels long." Carol pointed to the left, toward the smaller pens. "That helps prevent the horses from bunching up and possibly getting hurt." She watched the rogue protestor for a few moments. "At least that was true for the first group. Not sure how calming all that racket is."

"Let them go! They belong in the wild!"

The members of the Cloud Foundation gave each other an almost imperceptible nod. "Nice to meet you," Carol said. Then the three of them moved toward a small, white Subaru Outback wagon, climbed in, and drove away.

Bonnie looked at me and grinned. "Think I'll be going too, before it gets any more interesting."

"Yeah, probably a good idea," I agreed as the protestor continued her chanting.

"Well, I need a bit more information before I leave," Lulu said. "Need the cowboy's point of view. See ya." She slung the strap of her bag over her shoulder, pushed her glasses back into place, and headed for a group of wranglers huddled around the entrance of the catching pen. Bonnie went in the opposite direction and drove off in a small Toyota pickup. As I started toward the livestock trailer where Raven was waiting, a loud commotion began behind me. Looking back, I could see a few of the wranglers had surrounded the protestor and the rest, including Lulu DeLoure, were quickly advancing on her, the yelling and shouting getting louder and louder. *Oh this is not going to end well!*

I hurried around the backside of the large pen and reached the group just as some of the men were climbing over the top rail of the portable panels. "Hang on a minute, fellas," I said, holding up both hands. "Let's not get carried away."

"She's the one getting carried away," Nate shouted, stepping forward and pointing at the protestor. "Things were going just fine 'til she showed up! Now the mustangs are stirred up, and it's her fault."

"Yeah, her fault!" the rest of the wranglers chimed in.

"I have every right to be here," the protestor's voice blared through the speaker again, "and document the mistreatment of these animals."

"Mistreatment?" Nate yelled, moving even closer.

I stepped in between him and the target of his attack. "If you can get these guys to go back to handling the horses, I'll see if I can deal with her."

The way he stood there, glaring at the woman, I wasn't sure he was going to back down. Finally, he turned around. "All right, let's get the mustangs taken care of." Grabbing the crown of his cowboy hat and readjusting it on his head, he looked at me and muttered, "Somebody outta dump her ass out in the desert and see how she likes that." Then he spun around and followed the others, the overzealous reporter dogging his every step.

"Why don't we move back around there," I said, pointing to the area behind the large pen, "and let them regroup."

"I don't have to leave!" The speaker blasted her voice at me.

"Do you mind?" I pointed to the device strapped to her waist.

"Huh?" For a moment her close-set eyes, recessed under a pair of heavy eyebrows, seemed to lose their focus. The look was so comical, I had to bite the inside of my cheek to keep from laughing. "Oh sorry," she said when she finally understood what I meant and switched off the amplifier.

"My name's Sarah." I held out my right hand.

"Ida Dudley," she replied, ignoring my gesture and heading back the way she'd come.

"We can watch from here," I suggested when we reached the spot where Bonnie and I had been just moments ago. Without the chatter from Ida's amplifier, the wild horses did not seem as frantic, and the wranglers were able to separate and herd them toward the holding pens in small groups. "See how they're moving the horses? They aren't mistreating them at all."

Just then one of the larger animals broke from a group and rushed passed one of the wranglers. His horse shifted its weight back, spun quickly to the right, and lunged to block the escapee's route. It was a move I'd seen a cutting horse make many times while competing in high school rodeos, but this time, as the horse spun around, it bumped into a small yearling, knocking it down.

"Did you see that?" Ida yelled, pointing at the small horse as it struggled back onto its feet. Before I realized what she was doing, she'd switched her amplifier back on. "Animal cruelty!" Her voice exploded from the speaker, spooking the wild horses on our side of the pen and causing them to dart away. "Free the horses! Let them go!"

"Ida, stop that!" I demanded. "This isn't helping." The startled animals rushed around the pen, scattering the small groups the wranglers had managed to separate. The out-of-control protestor ignored me and began snapping pictures of the chaos. "In fact, it's making things worse," I said, as Nate threw down the rope he'd been using and stomped across the pen toward us. Lulu must have noticed him too because she began running around the outside of the pen, probably hoping to get a scoop on the action.

It was hot and getting hotter; I was sweaty and wishing I'd walked a little faster when I first decided to grab Raven and ride back to the trailer. But I hadn't, and now it looked like the situation was about to get completely out of hand.

I moved closer to Ida. "Look, you really need to stop this. If you don't, I'm afraid I'll have to do something to stop you."

She put her hands on her hips and leaned toward me. "And just how do you think you're going to do that?" Her voice erupted from the speaker.

Nate was just a few feet away from the side of the pen, so I knew I had to act fast. "Well you see," I began, trying to lead the protestor in the general direction of her car, "I'm a deputy sheriff and... "

"YOU'RE A DEPUTY?" Her expression and the way she looked me up and down were clear indicators that she didn't believe me.

I couldn't really blame her for doubting me, dressed in my cutoff sweats and baggy T-shirt and covered with cuts and bruises. But hearing it come through the amplifier must have made it slightly more convincing because it stopped Nate just as he reached the top of one of the portable panels, leaving him perched there like an overgrown vulture.

"Ida, please turn that off and listen to me for a minute."

Reluctantly, she complied and stood in front of me with her arms folded across her chest. "There's no way you're a deputy," she protested.

"She sure is," Lulu panted, having just arrived. "And a pretty good one at that, even if she doesn't look like one."

"Thanks, Lulu." *I think.* I glanced behind me and was relieved to see that Nate had climbed down and returned to the task of separating the wild horses. Turning my attention back to the protestor, I continued. "If you persist in using your personal amplifier and creating chaos for the wranglers, you will leave me no choice but to arrest you for disturbing the peace or being a public nuisance." The moment the words left my mouth I regretted saying them. I had no gun, no handcuffs, and more importantly, no patrol unit. If she called my bluff, I would have to tie her up with a borrowed rope and throw her on the back of my horse. "I really don't want it to come to that. They've almost got all the horses in the smaller pens and should start shipping them out soon."

"Oh no," Lulu said. "They aren't going to have the trucks come until tomorrow morning. That will let the horses settle down some more and rest before being loaded."

"Really?" Ida asked. "Tomorrow?"

Lulu nodded.

Without another word, the protestor that had caused so much trouble walked over to her car and got inside. After starting the engine, she rolled down the windows and drove away, country music blaring from her stereo.

"Apparently she likes everything loud," Lulu observed. "Well, gotta go. Have a story to write for next week's paper. See you later, Deputy." A moment later, she left in her faded red Pinto.

Not wasting another minute, I jogged across the dirt road and ducked behind the livestock trailer where Raven was waiting. "Come on, Boy. Let's get out of here."

I checked the cinch on the saddle, untied his lead rope, and climbed aboard. Prancing in place, my horse seemed as anxious as I was to head back up the hill.

I gave him his head as soon as we reached the dirt road, and he immediately settled into a fast trot. We'd traveled about a quarter mile when I heard hoofbeats behind me, coming up fast. Glancing over my right shoulder, I was surprised to see one of the wranglers gaining on me. I reined in my horse, and Nate swung around me until he was facing back down the hill.

"Just wanted to say thanks for getting rid of that pain in the ass. Don't know what you told her, but I never seen her leave before we were done."

"Glad I could help." I gave Raven's neck a vigorous rub. "And thank you for rescuing me earlier." When Nate didn't reply, I looked up. He was staring at something on the hillside behind me. I quickly scanned the area but didn't see anything out of the ordinary. "Uh, Nate?" I said when I faced him again.

"Huh, what?" His eyes refocused on me.

"Is everything okay?"

"Oh, yeah." His frown told me differently, but I didn't pursue it. "Guess I better get back." He touched the flat brim of his hat, signaled the sorrel with his spurs, and rode down the hill.

"Come on, Raven. Let's go home." The black gelding nodded his massive head, and we began the five-mile ride back to the trailer.

Chapter 5

"Mmm, what smells so good?" I called as I let myself in Remy's front door, my miniature mutt on my heels.

"Homemade biscuits." My neighbor placed the baking sheet he'd just removed from the oven onto the stovetop. Then he pulled out his blue and white handkerchief and mopped his sweaty face. "Too hot to be baking, but I wanted to try this here recipe. Look at these things." The biscuits were a golden brown and almost three inches high.

My mouth watered. "They look delicious."

"Came out of that cookbook I found at the old town hall here in Bidwell during the last valley wide yard sale. The civic club has one every year, raising money to restore the building." Remy reached for the small white binder he had propped up on his counter. "It's a bunch of recipes from folks right here in Surprise Valley." He flipped the book closed and shoved it over to me. A widower for several years and on the downhill side of retirement, Remy Hamilton was on a quest to duplicate his late wife's cooking.

"Hmm, this is great," I said, thumbing through the different sections. "Each tab has cooking hints and there are all kinds of recipes. Bet if I found my own copy, Pete wouldn't have anything bad to say about my cooking."

"Maybe," Remy said and then grinned at me through his white beard and mustache. "Anyway, thought these would go nice with the pot of beans I put on this morning."

He grabbed a large basket out of one of the cupboards and lined it with a white tea towel decorated with embroidered roosters. He piled it high with the freshly baked biscuits and folded the four corners over them. "Here, you take this," he said, handing it to me, "and as soon as I get this pot tied shut and grab my hat, we'll be ready to go with you."

"We?"

"Me and Millie of course. That way Bubba has someone to tussle with whilst we visit."

A few minutes later, we'd loaded the food and animals into the backseat of my Dooley and were pulling out of Remy's driveway, headed for County Road 1. "I need to make a quick stop before we start for Pete's," I said. Because I'd spent so much time at the wild horse roundup and worked on my secret contribution to dinner, I had yet to buy any beer. Fortunately, it was early enough as we drove through Fort Bidwell, the store on the corner of Bridge and Willow Streets was still open. I dashed inside and grabbed a bag of ice and a case of Miller Genuine Draft. Opening the ice chest I'd put in the bed of my truck, the pungent smell of chopped red onions rose from the large metal bowl covered with foil. Smiling, I placed the beer next to it, laid the ice on top, and closed the lid, certain that what was inside would change Pete's opinion of my cooking once and for all.

While Bubbles and Millie jockeyed for position at

either of the back windows, we rode in silence until we passed the Spaza Shop at Winje's Farm. "Have you ever been in there?" I asked Remy.

"Can't say as I have."

"I've been meaning to check it out, but I'm usually on patrol when I drive by during their business hours. I wonder what they sell in there?"

"Don't rightly know, but I 'spect we could check it out sometime."

I chuckled to myself. *There's that 'we' again.*

The aroma of beans and biscuits permeated the cab of the truck and made my stomach growl. Hoping to distract myself, I decided to have some fun with Remy. "Saw Bonnie earlier today."

"Who?"

"The biologist from the BLM, Bonnie Patterson."

Remy folded his arms across his chest. "Got nothing to say to her," he said.

I had to smile. After hiding a fawn I'd rescued so it wouldn't be taken away by the biologist, I was certain he didn't want to talk to her, but I couldn't resist teasing him. "I thought I might invite her over to your place one afternoon."

He glared at me. "You do that, and I won't have nothing to say to you neither."

I laughed. "Okay, okay. I was just kidding. How is Buck anyway?"

His whole demeanor changed instantly. "Growing like a weed. He's pert near twice as big as Millie here," he said, reaching back and scratching the top of the small goat's head. "No antlers yet—next year, maybe."

The next few miles passed quickly as he continued to tell me about the adventures of the orphaned fawn, which ended about the time we turned onto Laxaque Road. A quarter of a mile further, I pulled into Pete's narrow driveway and parked in front of the garage where he kept his '67 Pontiac GTO and '69 Harley-Davidson FLH Shovelhead, both of which he had restored himself.

"Don't see Shellie's rig," Remy said, opening the backdoor and freeing the two animals. I flashed on the first time I'd ever seen Shellie's Jeep; the color reminded me of purple Chiclets.

I walked to the back of the truck and dropped the tailgate. "I'm sure she'll be here in a few minutes." Although he'd never admit it, I was fairly certain Remy was quite fond of Shellie.

"She has to wait for her dessert to finish baking," Pete called as he came from his backyard—if you could really call it that. It consisted of a room-size piece of outdoor carpet that resembled short, fake grass, a round table with four matching chairs and an umbrella, and a very large, towable barbecue/smoker combo.

"What's she making?" I asked.

He took the ice chest from me. "She wouldn't tell me. Said it was a surprise."

I helped Remy get the rest of the food out of the Dooley, and the four of us followed Pete around his single-wide trailer.

"Got anything that needs to stay hot or cold?" he asked. "There's room in the fridge, or I can put it on the barbecue."

"It's warm enough I don't think the biscuits will get

cold but the beans might keep better if they stay hot," Remy said, holding up the pot he was carrying. "They probably should be stirred every now and again, so they don't stick."

I set the basket of biscuits on the table, under the umbrella. "There's something in the ice chest that should be kept cold."

"Yeah, beer is much better when it's cold." Pete grinned at me as he set the ice chest by the steps to the backdoor.

"Oh ha-ha, you're so funny." I stepped in next to him and faked a punch to his ribs before pulling the metal bowl out of the ice chest. "This is what needs to go in the fridge, and no peeking until dinner. Why don't you be useful and ice down the beer," I said, tromping up the stairs. "Remy, I'll get you a spoon while I'm in there if you'll keep an eye on Millie and Bubbles."

"Deal."

I'd been in Pete's house several times during the past few months, so I knew my way around. What I didn't know was how a single guy could keep it so neat. I'd never seen discarded clothes or shoes scattered across the floor or dirty dishes in the sink unlike Scott's place, which always looked like a bomb had gone off; my own house wasn't much better. Remy's house, on the other hand, was always neat and clean, but I attributed that to having been trained by his wife, Peggy, all those years ago.

Opening the door of the fridge, I spotted a place for the metal bowl and slid it onto the shelf next to a brightly colored fruit salad. *Even his fridge is neat!* I shut the door and pulled open the small drawer next to the stove. After locating a large spoon, I went back outside to find the two men sitting at the table, each enjoying a beer in the small amount of shade created by the umbrella. I snagged myself one out of the ice chest and joined them. "Here you go," I said, laying the spoon on the table in front of Remy.

"Let me have that, and I'll give 'em a stir for you. Gotta check the meat anyway." Pete grabbed the spoon and moved over to his barbecue. He gave Remy's beans a vigorous mixing and set the pot in the covered cooking compartment. Using the small towel that had been dangling from his hip pocket, he prodded a foil-wrapped package that was also inside, before closing the lid. Then he opened a second compartment mounted lower and to the left and poked at the remaining bed of red-hot coals with a small, short-handled shovel. "Should have just enough fire to finish this," he said, closing the curved door and returning to the table.

"That's quite the contraption you got there," Remy said, nodding at Pete's barbecue.

"It is sweet, isn't it? I designed it, and a buddy of mine helped me build it."

"Whatcha smokin' in there?" Remy asked.

Pete shook his head. "Not smoking anything. Barbecuing a brisket."

"Whatd'ya mean you ain't smoking? That there fire ain't under the meat; it's off to the side, and I seen smoke come out when you opened it."

"Yes, but true smoking can take days or weeks, and there's a cure involved. That brisket has a dry rub on it and—holy crap!"

"What's the matter?" I asked.

"I sound just like my dad," he said, shaking his head.

"That's a bad thing?"

"I guess you could call my dad a disciple of the almighty Texas barbecue."

"I thought he was a snake-handling preacher from Kentucky," I said.

Pete chuckled. "Yeah, that too. But the man knows his barbecue and shares that knowledge with everyone, willing or not, and apparently I just turned into my father. Anyway..." He checked his watch. "...the brisket has been in there for about twelve hours, and I should probably pull it out in the next few minutes."

"Twelve hours?" Remy and I chorused.

"Yeah, I got it all trimmed and in the 'cue when I got home after closing the bar."

"When did you sleep?" Remy asked,

"Haven't, really. Had to feed the fire every hour or so, so I took little catnaps." He grinned at us. "But if it turns out, it'll be worth it. So Remy, what do you think of my poor man's patio?"

"Makes sitting out here mighty tolerable, I 'spect."

"At least now we *can* sit out here," I said. "Before we put this together, he only had his towable barbecue, parked at the bottom of the stairs."

"It was handy that way, and there was a folding chair to sit on."

"Then this is a definite improvement," Remy said, holding up his beer as if making a toast.

The sound of a vehicle coming down the driveway interrupted our conversation. "That must be Shellie." Remy pushed himself out of his chair. "I'll go see if she needs any help." He stepped over the row of rocks we'd lined up along the edges of the outdoor carpet to hold it in place and disappeared around the end of Pete's mobile home.

"I think he's quite taken with Shellie," I whispered to Pete.

"And she's very fond of him, too," he replied. "Mentions something about the man every time she tends bar at the Spur. Reminds me of another couple I know." He winked at me before jumping up and lifting the lid on the covered cooking compartment. He stirred the beans again, pulled out the foil package and placed it on the grill at the other end. I was about to say something clever when the others, escorted by a dog and a goat, came around the corner and strolled toward the table.

Remy was carrying a striped casserole cozy, and Shellie, dressed in an ankle-length skirt and coordinating tee, had a fancy reusable shopping bag slung over one shoulder. "Where should I put this?" Remy asked.

"If we set it in the microwave," she began, setting her bag on the table, "then it should still be warm by the time we get around to dessert."

"What is it?"

She took the cozy from him. "A surprise." Then she hurried up the steps and slipped through the door.

Remy looked at Pete, who merely shrugged his shoulders before sitting down at the table. A minute or two later, Shellie came back out with four whiskey glasses, each one holding a single, large ice cube. "I've got something for you to try," she said, setting down the glasses and pulling a bottle out of her bag. "This Balvenie scotch is delicious." She ripped the paper off the top, pulled the cork, and deftly poured about an inch in each glass.

I picked up one and looked at the amber-colored liquid inside. "I don't really..."

"Don't try it yet," she scolded. "Swirl it and let the ice melt into it a bit." She demonstrated with her own glass, and the rest of us did the same. "This one has been aged for fourteen years in a rum cask. It's so smooth there's no burn; just amazing taste, with a hint of rum flavor."

Burn! That's what immediately comes to mind whenever I think of whiskey. In my rodeo days, the only ones I'd ever had access to were Jack Daniels or Jim Beam. I didn't mind a sip or two of Yukon Jack, and I'd tried a sarsaparilla whiskey and apple flavored Crown Royal before. But given a choice, I'd choose something other than whiskey.

"Okay," Shellie said, holding up her glass. "It should be ready to sample. Have a tiny first sip, give it a second or two and have another. That's when you get its true flavor." We all raised our glasses to our lips and took a small sip.

I'd tasted scotch only one other time, and it reminded me of old medicated Band-Aids. Although this scotch did not taste like that, I knew immediately I'd never manage another sip. It was nasty, burned all the way down my throat and kept on burning for several seconds. When the others went for sip number two, I did the same but kept my lips tightly together.

"Isn't it good?" Shellie asked.

"I'll say," Remy agreed. "It's one of the smoothest scotches I've had. And I've tossed back quite a few over the years."

"Pete?"

"Not bad."

"Sarah?"

"Um, well..." Frantically, I tried to think of something to say when Pete suddenly turned to me and asked, "So, how was training this morning?"

Oh, thank you! "The session itself was good until the wild horses showed up."

"What wild horses?" he and Remy asked in unison.

"Oh, that's right," Shellie said. "There was a wild horse roundup today, wasn't there?"

"Yes there was, and I got caught right in the middle of it."

"Let me guess..." Pete set down his glass and leaned back in his chair. "...you fell off your horse." His crystal-blue eyes twinkled with malicious mischief.

"No, I did not!" I exclaimed. "I was already on the ground, leading Raven."

"And?" He raised his eyebrows.

"And what?" I raised my own eyebrows.

"There just always seems to be an 'and' with you," he teased.

I glared at him for a second or two. "And..." I took a deep breath. "He ran off, and I had to chase after him," I blurted. Then I proceeded to share my adventure, which seemed to entertain the other three very much. "And just when I think things are going to get out of hand, that crazy protestor gets in her car and drives off, with some country song about wild ponies in Storey County blaring from her stereo."

Shellie started laughing. "Oh dear, that's Lacey J. Dalton's song 'Let 'Em Run.' I was listening to it the other day. In fact, I think it's in my Jeep right now." She put her hands on the arms of her chair. "I can go get it if you want."

"That's okay," I said, holding up my free hand in surrender, "I've had my fill of wild horses and the people involved with them."

"Okay then," she chuckled and settled back into her chair. "When do we eat?"

"Somebody grab the beans and bring them inside. I'll slice the brisket, and we can fill our plates and come back out here to eat." Pete snagged the foil package off the grill, and the rest of us followed him inside.

"Go ahead and set out the other food, while I do this," he said, placing the package on a large, white cutting board he'd laid across the sink earlier.

"Why, that there piece of meat is burnt!" Remy declared as he watched Pete peel back the foil.

"That's the bark you're looking at. It's supposed to look like that."

"Bark? On meat? And how in tarnation can it get so burnt wrapped in foil?"

"This is true Texas barbecue, Remy," Pete explained as he began cutting the brisket into thick slices. "The smoke gives it its color, and once the meat has absorbed the amount you want, wrapping it in foil helps finish the cooking process." He cut off a small piece, balanced it on the end of his knife, and offered it to Remy.

He hesitated, looked at me, and then placed the bite-size piece of meat in his mouth. As he chewed in silence, Pete handed Shellie and me our own pieces to try. It was unlike any beef I have ever tried; juicy, slightly sweet and so tender it practically melted in my mouth.

"This is absolutely..."

"Delicious!" Remy interjected.

Shellie nodded in agreement, savoring her own bite.

"Now," Pete said, surveying the row of containers Shellie and I had arranged on the counter, "let's see what's in here." He lifted the foil on my metal bowl and peered inside. "You cooked?"

Chapter 6

Shellie gave us a quick wave before climbing into her Jeep and driving away. While I said good-bye to Pete, Remy opened the back door of the Dooley for two very dusty, tired animals. Climbing in and laying back in the driver's seat, my extremely long and busy day finally hit me, and I closed my eyes.

"Well, that sure was a nice time," Remy said after he'd settled into his own seat. He rubbed his temporarily enlarged belly. "Don't recollect the last time I ate that much!"

"I know what you mean. Probably should've had only one serving of dessert myself." Starting the engine, I made a mental note to add at least twenty minutes onto my next workout with my sparring dummy.

"That peach cobbler was wonderful, wasn't it. I haven't had one that tasty since my Peggy passed," he said, ceremoniously removing his felt hat and placing it over his heart. "And that potato salad of yours was mighty good too," he added a moment later, replacing his hat and fastening his seatbelt.

I slid the gearshift into reverse and slowly let out the clutch. "Yes it was," I agreed, grinning with immense satisfaction.

The ride from Pete's through Cedarville was quiet, except for a faint snoring sound. I couldn't tell if it was coming from Remy or one of the animals curled up in the backseat. We'd almost reached the small airport when the chirp of my cell phone broke the silence.

Grabbing it from the cupholder in the center console, I simultaneously stepped on the brake and clutch and glided to the side of the road.

"Murdock."

"Hey, Sarah. It's Ira from dispatch."

"Hello, Ira. What's up?"

"I got a call about an abandoned vehicle over at Rabbit Traxx, and the guy wants someone to get over there as soon as possible."

Give me a break! I checked the clock on the dashboard and understood why I felt so tired. It was almost ten o'clock. "What's so urgent? Can't it wait 'til morning?"

There was a short pause. "He sounded pretty freaked out, and I'd be willing to bet he'll keep calling until someone shows up."

"Fine. I'll go." I snapped my phone shut and tossed it back into the cupholder. "Damn it!"

"What's going on?" Remy asked with way more enthusiasm than I was feeling.

"Oh, the guy over at Rabbit Traxx is complaining about some car that apparently is abandoned and wants someone to come check it out."

"Well, the way I see it, you're a lot closer now than if you was to be at home."

I chuckled as I finished my three-point turn and

headed back toward Cedarville. The man always had a way of looking at the positive side of any situation.

"And I get to tag along!"

Of course! There's that, too.

Five minutes later, I swung into the gas station on the corner of Patterson and Townsend Streets. The attendant I knew only as Mike was pacing back and forth along the row of pumps furthest from the entrance. I pulled into a parking space next to the building and got out.

He crossed the lot toward me. "I'm sorry but we're closed."

"Hey Mike," I said. "So what's going on?"

"Oh Deputy, I didn't see it was you." He removed his wire rim glasses. Cleaning them with the bottom of his polo work shirt, he shook his head. "This whole thing is a little unsettling."

"Why would an abandoned car be unsettling?" Remy demanded.

I leaned toward him. "Let me deal with this," I whispered.

"Okay, okay." He folded his arms across his chest.

"What's unsettling..." Mike replaced his glasses and glared at Remy. "...is that the abandoned car seemed to be fueling itself."

Must be more tired than I thought. "I'm sorry, did you say it was fueling itself?"

"Yes, I did!" He pointed toward a small, silver car parked close to where he'd been pacing. "I was in the backroom getting a box of napkins off the top shelf. When I carried it out to the counter, I noticed the car. I hustled out to help the customer, but there wasn't one. The nozzle was stuck into the tank, the door was hanging open, and the pump was running. I figured maybe they were using the restroom, so I finished filling the tank, closed the door and went inside. Several minutes go by and no one comes out, so I got nervous. I knocked on each door and went inside, but nobody was there. It was only after I had looked everywhere that I called the Sheriff's Office."

"That is mighty peculiar," Remy said, reaching up under his hat and scratching his head.

We walked over to get a closer look. The car was a dusty, Nissan Sentra with Colorado plates. It seemed vaguely familiar somehow, but I thought maybe it was because the make and model were fairly common. As I moved around the vehicle a second time, Remy peered through the passenger window. "Looks like there's one of those newfangled radios in here. What are they called?" He snapped his fingers a couple of times. "Boss?"

"You mean Bose?" I asked.

He grinned and shook his index finger at me. "Yeah, that's it."

"Oh shit!"

"What?"

"I think I know who's missing?"

"You do?" Remy and Mike said together.

"Ida Dudley!"

"Who's Ida Dudley?" Mike looked at me and then Remy.

"Yeah, who's Ida..." Remy stopped, tilted his head to one side and the spark of realization lit up his face. "The crazy protestor?"

I nodded.

"But how?"

I shrugged. "No idea." I started back toward my Ford to retrieve my cell phone and hopefully find some kind of notebook and something to write with. I'd almost reached it when I spotted someone coming from one of the houses across the street. As soon as I realized it was a woman, I experienced a brief moment of relief, but as she got closer, it quickly faded.

Dressed in flip-flops, purple leggings, and an oversized floral T-shirt, she appeared closer to Remy's age than my own and looked nothing like the missing person. "What's all the excitement going on over here?" she asked, whisking her long, salt-and-pepper hair into a bun and securing it with a large hair tie that matched her shirt.

"Evening, ma'am. I'm Deputy Murdock, and I'm just checking on a vehicle for Mike over there." I pointed toward the row of pumps.

"Usually things are pretty quiet around here on a Sunday, but with all the traffic that's been in and outta here tonight, I figured there was something going on."

"Traffic?"

"Oh, yeah. There's been a couple of cars come through here—besides that one." She nodded toward the Nissan. "A truck with an animal hauler pulled in right behind it. He didn't stay but a minute, though. Guess he didn't like the prices or something."

"Would you mind waiting here for just a moment?" I asked. "I'd like to grab my notebook, so I can write this down."

"Not at all. Harold's watching his program. He won't even notice I'm gone."

I ransacked the center console and found my gas mileage log and a fairly dull stubby pencil. Returning to where the woman was waiting, I flipped to a blank page. "Can you describe the vehicles you saw tonight?"

"Sure. The first car was red, the second one was a dark brown. The truck pulling the trailer was a dark blue or black, and the trailer was a light color—white or silver, I think."

"Did you notice if it was a Ford or Chevy or maybe a Dodge?"

"Oh heavens no," she said raising her right arm and flicking her hand at me. "Harold knows that stuff, not me."

"Did he happen to see the truck?"

"He don't see nothing when his program is on."

I jotted down the color of the truck and trailer. "When it pulled in, did the engine make a lot of noise?"

She shook her head. "Sorry. TV's too loud to hear anything else."

So much for any useable information! "I see. May I have your name for my report?"

"Mabel. Mabel Swanson."

I wrote that on the next line. "Thank you. And if I need any other information you live..."

"In that blue house, right there." She pointed across the street.

"Got it. Thanks again." As Mabel headed back home, I grabbed my phone and went back over to the car. I mentally cringed when I heard Remy telling Mike all about being my partner. I hit the redial button and wrote down the license plate number while I waited for Ira to answer.

"Hi, Sarah. So what did you find?"

"I need you to run a Colorado plate for me."

"Okay, shoot." I read off the numbers and then wait- ed. "It comes back for a 1994 Nissan Sentra registered to a Idaleen Agnes Dudley out of Denver. Hold on and I'll run her license." Another pause. "She doesn't have any outstanding warrants, but she has been arrested a time or two for disturbing the peace."

No surprises there! "Can you print me out a copy of her picture? Leave it there at the desk and I'll pick it up in the morning." I thought about what Mabel had told me. "Put out an APB on her, and call Bert over at the motel. Ask him to meet me here early in the morning with his flatbed tow truck. Say around seven o'clock."

"Will do." He disconnected, and I slipped my phone into my back pocket.

"Well, it's confirmed. This is Ida's car."

"So now what?" Remy asked.

"We'll haul it back to the SO tomorrow, and..."

Mike interrupted me. "What's the SO?"

"Sheriff's Office," Remy answered in his most official voice.

"Are the keys in it?" I asked, opening the driver side door.

Mike stared at me for a second or two. "I'm not sure. I didn't look." As I slid in behind the wheel, Mike and Remy crowded around the open door.

The first thing to get my attention was an air freshen- er depicting a small group of horses running along some shore. Right above that, a small effigy of a running horse hung from the rearview mirror. Blankets and a couple of pillows filled the backseat, and the entire floor of the vehicle was hidden by a layer of wadded paper and discarded food containers that had to be at least a foot deep.

"Looks to me like she's been living in this here car," Remy said.

"I think you're right." I leaned slightly to the right and spotted the keys dangling from the ignition. "Is it okay to leave it parked over by the building for the night?"

"Sure, sure. That'll be fine." Mike stepped back a few feet.

I turned the key and was immediately deafened by the music blaring from the car's stereo. Both men jumped back as I frantically fumbled with the knobs in search of the off button. Finally, the music ceased, and we all let out a huge sigh.

"Well, that was exciting," I said before closing the door and moving the car to a parking space next to my truck. After making sure the emergency brake was on, I got out and locked the door.

"Ain't you gonna check the trunk?" Remy asked.

"Probably leave that to whoever logs it in tomorrow."

"Well," he began, "I heard tell of a story about a guy that got robbed at gunpoint and then got tied up and tossed into the trunk of his own car. Took three days for anyone to look inside, and he was pert near dead."

Having almost been locked in a trunk myself not so long ago, I was more than willing to test his hypothesis. "Okay, Remy. We'll check the trunk." The three of us moved to the rear of the vehicle, and I slid the key into the lock and gave it a turn to the right. The inside was just as disorderly as the rest of the car, only with articles of clothing rather than trash. "Satisfied?" I asked and then slammed the lid shut.

"What if she shows up? Don't need nothing destroyed if she decides to break in looking for her keys," Mike said.

"Okay." I thought for a minute. "If you have some tape, I'll write her a note explaining that I have the keys, and I'll leave my phone number."

"Good enough. I'll be right back."

While Mike was inside, I scribbled a note to Ida on a page of my notebook and tore it out. A few minutes later, we were once again headed north on County Road 1.

Chapter 7

Bubbles woke me up twenty minutes before my alarm was scheduled to go off with an urgent request to go outside. By the time I returned to my bedroom, the alarm was wailing and my day had begun.

I dumped a handful of food into the dog's dish, which he ignored, most likely holding out for something better at Remy's. I'd gotten into the habit of taking my dust mop of a dog with me on patrol, sort of a miniaturized canine unit, but with the onset of the recent heat wave, I figured he was better off romping with Millie.

Forty-five minutes later, I was showered and dressed with plenty of time to meet the tow truck. Grabbing a protein bar and a bottle of water, I promised myself a large coffee-to-go from the Wagon Wheel Café when I got to Cedarville.

Taking advantage of the cooler early morning temperature, I cruised south with the front windows down. Thirty minutes later, I pushed through the door of the café, the bell tinkling as it banged against the glass, and sat at my usual spot at the counter covered with vintage pink and green Formica.

"What can I get you, Hon?" Sal asked, sliding her pen from the mass of brassy blond hair she wore piled on top of her head. Sal—short for Sally—was the only person I'd ever seen waiting tables. Dressed in her pink waitress uniform and white sensible shoes, she claimed not to be a day over 60, but I had the feeling she had been saying that for some time now.

"Just a large coffee-to-go with the works," I replied.

"Already had something to eat?"

I chuckled. "No, but I have to meet someone in just a few minutes." She clicked her tongue at me as she poured my coffee.

A few minutes later, I arrived at the gas station just seconds before Bert pulled his flatbed tow truck into the parking lot. Bert Evans runs a towing service out of his tire shop in Alturas. He also owns the Stony Ridge Lodge, where I lived when I first came back to California, and he's Cindy's uncle.

"Whatcha got going this morning?" he called as he lowered his substantial body out of the cab of his truck.

"Missing person. Seems she came into the station last night to fuel up and then vanished. This is her car," I said, pointing to the silver Nissan, "so I need it hauled back to the office. I'll call Josh after we get it loaded and let him know it's on the way."

"Seems easy enough." He adjusted his sweat-stained ball cap. "That is, if you got the keys."

I pulled them out of the front pocket of my pants and jangled them. "Right here."

Bert grinned as he took them and got started.

I stuck around, helping when necessary, until the car was on the flatbed and ready to be tied down. After topping off my own tank, I bade Bert good-bye and headed for the end of Highway 299.

Pulling up to the four-way stop in the center of Cedarville, I pushed the preset button on my phone and called the office. "Hi Cindy," I said when she answered, "put me through to Josh, would you?"

"Lab."

"Hey Josh, it's Sarah. I've got a silver Nissan coming your way. Belongs to a possible missing person. Give it the once over for me and let me know if you find anything out of the ordinary."

"Sure thing."

"Thanks." I started to lower the phone from my ear but suddenly remembered. "Oh, and by the way, I may have killed my personal radio."

"How did you manage that? Those things are pretty indestructible."

"Took it for a swim."

"What the hell, Sarah!"

"It's a long story. I'll fill you in later today. Do you think you can find me another one?"

"I'll look around and see what I can scrounge up for you."

"Thanks, Josh."

"Later."

I disconnected and continued driving east. When I arrived at the temporary holding pens the wranglers had set up the day before, the horses were quietly nibbling on some hay that had been thrown out for them. *Much calmer than yesterday.*

The livestock trailers that had been lined up on the other side of the road were gone as were the pickups that pulled them. Only the semitruck that hauled the panels was there. As I parked next to it, I spotted a lone wrangler on the far side of the pens. He must have seen me as well because he came right over.

"Can I help you with something, Deputy?" he asked.

"Hello Earl," I said.

He frowned at me for a moment until he recognized me. "Well, howdy. I didn't realize it was you."

I seem to get that a lot. "You here alone?"

"Yeah. I drew watch duty last night. Had to sleep on the truck." He nodded toward the semitruck where a rumpled sleeping bag was rolled out on the deck of the trailer.

"Did anyone show up out here last night?"

He slowly shook his head.

"Any rigs drive by? Say, maybe a truck and trailer?"

Earl began shifting his weight from one foot to the other. "Well...um." His eyes darted around.

"Oh come on, Earl. It's wide open. You'd be able to see any vehicle that came by from anywhere. Did somebody drive by?"

"I think so," he murmured.

"What do you mean you think so?"

Finally, he let out a huge sigh. "I was in the crapper!"

I glanced around and spotted the familiar portable outhouse. "You're telling me that you were here all alone and you didn't open the door to check?"

He shook his head again. "Door's on the back side."

I looked at the small, blue hut again, and sure enough, the door was on the side facing away from the road. "So you *did* hear something go by?"

He nodded.

"But you don't know what?"

He shook his head.

"Okay, fine. Thanks." I started back toward my patrol unit. Just as I reached for the door, I heard some vehicle dropped off the pavement and onto the dirt portion of the highway, creating quite a ruckus.

"There! That there is the sound I heard!" Earl exclaimed, rushing toward me.

Looking back toward Cedarville, I saw a dark blue Chevy Silverado towing an empty white livestock trailer slow down and park on the other side of the road.

"Good morning," Nate called as he climbed out. "Did you come to watch us load the horses?"

"Not exactly," I said, walking over to meet him. "I'm looking into a missing person case."

"Oh? Who's missing?"

"Ida Dudley."

"Really?" He chuckled. "Well, I say good riddance."

"Oh, come on man," Earl said, pulling on the brim of his cowboy hat.

"I'm serious. That woman has been nothing but a pain in the ass. Hell, she's the reason that 'ol..." He stopped and shook his head.

"Go on," I urged, hoping to gather any possible information.

"Nah, don't matter." He tugged on the waistband of his jeans. "Come on Earl, we've got work to do." He headed back toward his rig, so I tagged along.

He swung open the back door of the livestock trailer and climbed in. Earl stood just outside and waited. While Nate handed him a couple of lassos and a short whip with a white flag attached to the tip, I peeked inside.

Spotless! "Wow, this has got to be the cleanest trailer I've ever seen."

"I hosed it out this morning," Nate said as he stepped down and closed the door.

"Did you fuel up last night?" I asked.

"No, did that this morning, too. Just before coming out. Why?"

"Oh, no reason." As we crossed the road again, I noticed more rigs approaching on 299. "So, Earl tells me he had to sleep out here to keep an eye on things. Where did the rest of you stay?"

"Our boss made arrangements for us to stay at the fairgrounds. That way we could turn our horses out in a corral."

"Speaking of horses, won't you need yours today?"

"Won't need all of them." He extended his left thumb and jabbed it over his shoulder. "A couple of the guys brought theirs, in case one of the mustangs makes a break for it, but most of the loading is done on foot."

"I see. And what did you guys do to pass the time last night?"

When we reached the large catching pen, Nate rested his forearms on one of the panels, placed his right foot on a lower cross bar, and watched the horses mill around in the smaller pens for a few moments. "After grabbing a bite to eat, we played cards for awhile and then hit the hay. It'd been a long day." He slid his foot off the bar and turned to face me. "What's with all the questions?"

"Look Nate," I began, "I'm going to be straight with you. A rig matching yours was seen at the gas station just before Ida disappeared."

"Oh," he said, nodding his head. All of a sudden, there was a flash of understanding, and then it was gone.

"Something wrong?"

He muttered something under his breath that I couldn't quite make out as he watched the other wranglers park their rigs and move toward the pens. "Look," he said abruptly, "I need to get these guys lined out. The transport trucks will be here anytime, and we need to have these animals ready to go. Is there anything else you need?"

I wasn't sure. I wasn't sure Nate was telling the truth. I wasn't sure if the truck and trailer had anything to do with the fact that Ida Dudley was missing—if she really was missing. For all I knew, it could be some kind of publicity or sympathy stunt. All I could do was follow what few leads I had and hope for the best.

"I'd like to get statements from you and your crew. Can you come to the Sheriff's Office in Alturas later today? I can arrange to have another deputy help out, so it shouldn't take too long."

"By the time we get the horses loaded and everything torn down and put back on the semi, it's gonna be pretty late in the afternoon. How about first thing in the morning on our way home? We should be passing through around nine."

"That'll be fine. The office is right on Main Street as you come into town." I pulled out my new notebook and a pen. "Here, write down your name and contact info for me—just in case."

Nate complied and so did the rest of the men. While I waited for each one to scribble in my notebook, I gathered as much information as I could through casual conversation. One by one, they corroborated Nate's story, so either he was telling the truth or they all were in on it. I still wasn't sure.

The coolness of morning had burned off when I climbed into my patrol unit, so I rolled up my windows and cranked up the air conditioning, not envying the wranglers and the job ahead of them one little bit. As I left, I looked for a rig with the same color scheme as Nate's but did not see one. The trailers ranged in color from red to black and most of the trucks were white or beige.

The inside of the Ford Explorer had cooled down nicely by the time I passed the High Desert Hot Springs on my way back to Cedarville. When I reached Main Street, my stomach growled, reminding me I'd skipped breakfast, so I pulled up to the Wagon Wheel Café again for something with a little more sustenance than a large coffee.

Busier than my first visit, most of the spots at the counter were taken, including mine, which was occupied by one of Nate's wranglers.

"Aren't you late?" I asked, sliding into the seat next to him.

He frowned at me. "Huh?"

"The rest of the crew are already out at the pens."

"Oh, yeah." He dropped what was left of his piece of toast onto his plate, slapped down a ten dollar bill, and left.

"What was that about?" Sal asked, stopping in front of me just long enough to fill a clean cup with coffee and set out a napkin and set of silverware.

"I told him the rest of his buddies were already working."

"Buddies?"

"Yeah. They've corralled some wild horses at the end of 299 and are shipping them out today."

"Oh, you mean the rent-a-cowboys. At least that's what they call themselves." She grabbed a pot of coffee and made the rounds, topping off cups for patrons that wanted more. "But he wasn't one of them boys," she said when she came back to the counter.

"He wasn't?"

"Nuh-uh. Now what'll ya have?" She poised her pen over her pad.

I ordered the standard breakfast of bacon and eggs with hash browns and toast. While I waited, I took out my notebook and made a list of things I needed to do in the next couple of days. I'd just finished when Sal plopped my plate in front of me. A dash of hot sauce, a couple squirts of ketchup, and a generous dollop of blackberry jam, it was ready to consume, which I did in near record time. Then I paid my check, left Sal a nice tip, and stepped outside.

Swearing the temperature had increased by another ten degrees, I sought refuge in my rig. With the air conditioner set on maximum, I headed south toward the fairgrounds.

Chapter 8

I turned right onto Locust Street and approached the entrance to the fairgrounds. Staying to the left, I eased past the main buildings toward the grandstands. After parking in the shade of the farthest tree, I grabbed my cell phone and got started on my list.

"Hey, Cindy. It's Sarah," I said when she answered my call with her typical Sheriff's Office greeting.

"Oh hi, Sarah."

"Can you do me a couple of favors, please?"

"Sure, what do you need?"

"First of all let Josh know I won't be coming in today, but I'll be there tomorrow for sure."

"Okay?"

Her intonation told me she wanted more information. "He's supposed to be getting me a new radio since I fried mine going in after our 'drowning victim' last week."

She giggled. "Oh, yeah."

The interior of my patrol unit was starting to heat up, so I gave the ignition a quarter turn and rolled down my windows. It didn't help much. "Ira was supposed to print out a picture and leave it for me at the desk. Do you see it anywhere?"

The sound of rustling paper came over the line. "Here it is," Cindy said, "it was folded—aaaaa!"

"What's the matter?"

"The woman in this picture looks like she's insane!"

I flashed on my own reaction the first time I saw Ida. "You think so, huh?"

"Yes! The wild-eyed expression, the disarray of hair around her face."

"Well, she's my missing person." I rubbed the twin creases above the bridge of my nose with the first two fingers of my free hand and took a deep breath. "So, I'm going to see if someone from the *Alturas Gazette* will come get that picture and run some kind of article in this week's paper."

"Do you really think anyone's going to do that?"

"I believe I know just the person that will. Oh that reminds me, will you reserve both interrogation rooms for me starting at nine in the morning? Probably need them for a couple of hours."

"Gotcha."

"And since I'll probably be in the office most of the morning, do you want to do lunch?"

"You bet. Dirk is getting ready for some exposition he's attending next week, so I'm wide open."

I felt myself grimace. Dirk Sandusky was the undersheriff and a pompous womanizing ass! An FBI reject, he especially had it in for me and had given me cause to beat up the garbage can in the ladies' restroom more than once. "Great. See you then."

I snapped my phone shut and got out of the Explorer. My shirt was soaked with sweat, and a faint breeze brought some relief from the heat but not much. Opening my phone again, I began scrolling through my contacts until I found the name I was searching for and hit the dial button.

"Gazette," the voice on the other end said.

"Miss DeLoure, please."

A familiar giggle and then, "One moment."

"This is Lulu."

"Hi Miss DeLoure. Deputy Murdock."

"Oh hi, Deputy. Please, call me Lulu. What can I do for you?"

"Well..." I paused and reconsidered what I was about to do. Without any evidence and only one possible lead, I figured it couldn't hurt. "I am working on a case and need you to run a picture in the paper for me."

"Okay, what picture?"

"Go by the Sheriff's Office and talk to the dispatcher, Cindy. She has the picture, and it will need to say something like 'Have you seen this person? If so contact...'" I rattled off the phone number for the office and my own cell number.

"Got it. So is this person wanted for some heinous crime?"

Oh, brother! "No, apparently she is missing."

"Oh." Her voice dripped with disappointment.

"Can you make sure it gets in this week's paper?"

There was a pause. "Well, I don't know. They're working on the pages now."

I needed some leverage. "Remember that protestor out at the roundup yesterday?"

"Yes?"

"Well, her car was found abandoned at the gas station in Cedarville last night."

"You mean she's vanished?"

"Yeah, something like that. So, if you help me get her picture in the paper, you'll be the first to know when, and if, this woman shows up, no matter what the circumstances are."

"You mean I'll be the first one you call to cover the story?"

"Absolutely."

"Okay, I'm on it!" And she disconnected.

Certain that was going to come back and bite me in the butt, I made a third phone call.

"Hi Scott," I said when the call went through.

"Well howdy, Sarah. What's up? Got any dead bodies ya need help with?"

"No, nothing like that but I could use your help tomorrow morning taking statements."

"Oh?"

"Yeah. I have about twenty cowboys I need to interview."

"Uh, well, I don't know. I got a big area to patrol tomorrow and..."

"Look," I interrupted. "I just need you to record half of these guys answering some questions I'll have written out. And I'll take care of all the paperwork."

"Okay, deal. What time?"

"Nine o'clock."

"See ya then." And he disconnected.

I snapped my phone shut again, moved to the back of my rig, and snagged a bottle of water out of the case

I'd tossed in there last week. Sipping the tepid water, I strolled toward the livestock area. The wranglers' horses were milling around in a corral at the west end of the show arena. Wandering around the animal barns, I spotted a wash station and a couple piles of feculence that may have been cleaned out of a livestock trailer.

I looked around and found a piece of discarded rebar in the weeds next to the fence. Using it, I probed the mess, hoping no one would see me poking through a pile of horse manure. Unable to find anything unusual, I put the rebar back where I found it and headed to the Explorer.

With nothing more to do until tomorrow, I returned to my normal duties and began patrolling south toward Eagleville. Just past the tiny town, I turned left onto Hays Canyon Road and headed due east toward the border. As I passed the small, dirt airstrip, I considered all the remote ways and alternative modes of transportation to get in and out of this valley. A person could virtually vanish, never to be seen again.

When I reached Nevada, I turned around and headed back toward Eagleville. Halfway, I turned right onto County Road 37 and drove through sagebrush and juniper trees and again headed toward the border. On the way back, I veered right again, eventually traveling along the eastern shore of Cambron Lake, which looked like it hadn't seen a drop of water for a very long time. The shimmer of heat waves radiating up from the asphalt as I pulled back onto the paved road told me the temperature had risen significantly.

Planning the rest of my patrol in my head, I backtracked to the Eagleville General Store. I had to chuckle when I saw the small changeable letter sign hanging above the entrance, which read "Bullets and Booze." *A scary combination for sure but guaranteed to catch the eye of passersby!* I quickly selected a few things for a snack later in the afternoon in what I hoped would be a cooler location. After grabbing a couple more waters out of the back, I again headed south on County Road 1.

A quarter of an hour later, I'd driven around Lower Lake and through a small corner of Lassen County before reaching Nevada. The landscape all looked the same, high desert sand dotted with sagebrush and small juniper trees. Definitely not a place to get stranded, and I was glad I had a full tank of gas.

Turning around, I traveled north as far as Patterson Mill Road, which I followed until I reached the north end of Sworinger Reservoir. A popular spot with bass fishermen, it is fed by three or four creeks that run out of the Warner Mountains. The water level, however, was quite a bit below the high water mark this time of year. Spotting a dark grey GMC pickup parked along the shore on the backside of the reservoir, I decided to drive closer and take a look.

The pickup had been backed up right to the edge of the water, and a faded patio umbrella had been stuck into one of the rear stake pockets. After parking my rig so it was blocking the other vehicle, I climbed out into the heat and walked around to the far side. The driver was hunkered down in an old lawn chair within the small circle of shade created by the umbrella, his legs stretched out in front of him and a fishing pole in his hand.

"Morning," I said as I approached.

"Morning," the man said, not moving a muscle.

"Mind if I take a look at your fishing license?" I asked, taking a couple steps closer.

Without saying a word, the man quickly reached inside his fishing vest, and my hand instinctively moved to the butt of my Sig 9mm. When he produced a small, clear plastic pouch and held it out, I exhaled, unaware I'd been holding my breath.

Stepping into the patch of shade, I found the slight decrease in temperature a welcomed change, but it was still hot. I took the pouch and flipped it over so I could read the name. "Edward Flowers."

"That's me," he said.

I looked at the man again. It was difficult to see his face because of the ball cap he had pulled down over his eyes, and the full beard didn't look familiar, but the voice fit the owner of the High Desert Hot Springs I'd met over six months ago during my first murder case as deputy in Surprise Valley.

"Nice beard, Ed," I said, handing back his license.

He leaned to the right and looked at me over his left shoulder. "Did you come to arrest me?"

"Arrest you?"

He turned back around and stared at the dark green water of the reservoir. "It had to be done; I just couldn't stand all that racket another second." He shook his head. "Abby told me to let her be, but I couldn't help myself. I hitched up the trailer, shoved her inside, and drove off."

Omigod! My hand moved toward my gun again. I couldn't believe what I was hearing. "Ed," I said slowly, "where did you take her?"

"Gotta be honest, I thought about taking her to the slaughterhouse." He set his pole on the ground and heaved himself out of his chair. The back of his brown T-shirt was soaked with sweat. He removed his hat and swiped the beads of moisture off his brow with his forearm before replacing it. "Abby said she'd call the sheriff. I just didn't think she'd actually do it." He took a step toward me.

"Ed! Where did you take Ida?"

He frowned at me. "Who's Ida?"

"The woman you hauled off in your livestock trailer!"

"Deputy, it may be this heat, but I don't have any idea what you're talking about."

"But you just told me you shoved her into your trailer and drove off."

Ed chuckled. "That was a jenny."

More than one?! "Jenny who?"

"Not Jenny—a jenny. You know, a female donkey." He shook his head again. "Abby heard about this donkey needing a home, so she arranged to have it dropped off at the resort. Only it's too young, so it brays all the time. I haven't had a decent night's sleep for days." He laughed. "What on earth made you think I'd hauled some woman off?" He stepped over to the dropped tailgate of his truck, slid open a small ice chest and retrieved two bottles of water, one of which he offered to me.

"Well, I've got this missing person," I began, taking the bottle and twisting off the top. I took a couple huge swallows of the ice-cold water. "And I have reason to believe she was taken away in a livestock trailer, so when you started talking about taking 'her' away I…"

"You thought I had done it," Ed interjected.

Shrugging my shoulders slightly, I grinned at him and nodded.

"Who is this woman, anyway?"

"Oh some protestor that showed up at the wild horse roundup yesterday."

"So then the missus didn't call the sheriff?" he asked.

"Not that I'm aware of, Ed." I finished off my bottle of water. "So, how's the fishing?"

"Hell, I don't know. Threw out my line awhile ago and haven't checked it. Mostly just waiting for Abby to calm down before I go home."

Not envying his return home, I had to smile. I'd seen Abigail Flowers in action—not her temper necessarily, but her ability to control a situation. "Well, I wish you luck." I returned to my patrol unit and headed back to the main road. Half an hour later, I turned left onto Emerson Road and began the three-mile climb to the campground, which is nestled among Jeffrey pines and juniper trees.

First thing I did when I got there was cruise through and see who was around. Like the one near Cave Lake in the northern end of Surprise Valley, it is dry camping and free of charge. Only two sites were occupied, but since it was a popular spot with deer hunters and the season was due to start the following week, I suspected it would fill up soon. Finding a picnic table in a shady spot, I pulled into a nearby camping space and got out.

The air felt twenty degrees cooler thanks to a significant breeze traveling through the trees. I grabbed my snack and strolled over to the table. Sitting backwards and using the table as a backrest, I pushed my sunglasses onto the top of my head and placed my elbows on the surface behind me, glad to escape the heat I'd been enduring on the valley floor. I was just sorry I hadn't brought Bubbles along as he would've thoroughly enjoyed exploring the campground. It also might be fun to come stay a few days with Raven and do some leisurely exploring—after hunting season, of course.

As I munched on some beef jerky and a crisp, sweet apple, I thought about the shady spot next to the creek that runs through my property and promised myself to spend the remainder of the afternoon there. All I had to do was get through the rest of my patrol and peel off my sweat-soaked uniform the instant I got home. I still had to come up with a list of questions for tomorrow but decided I could do that first thing in the morning before heading for the office.

Checking my watch, I figured it'd be after two-thirty by the time I reached Cedarville and then take another thirty minutes to drive to Fort Bidwell, cruising along in an air-conditioned vehicle. *Good way to end the day.* With trash in hand, I strolled back to my unit and headed home.

About two miles south of Cedarville, I vaguely remembered passing some kind of vehicle when something smacked the base of my windshield followed by a loud thumping sound. Certain I'd blown a tire, I pulled over as quickly as I could and got out. Walking around to the passenger side of my patrol unit, I was amazed to find a work boot dangling by one of its laces from the windshield wiper. Glancing back the way I had come, I spotted a service truck of some kind just before it vanished around a turn. I jerked the boot loose, jumped back in and began chasing the vehicle.

Within a mile, I caught up to it and hit my lights. It took another mile before the driver realized I was there and pulled over. I radioed the stop into dispatch and approached what I recognized as a sewage truck, as evidenced by the portable outhouse on the back.

"Afternoon Deputy," the man said when I reached his open window. He ran his left hand over his mostly bald head and wiped the moisture it had collected on the front of his tan work shirt, leaving a wet streak behind.

"Afternoon," I replied. "Where you headed?"

"Eagleville. Got another john to pick up at the picnic area. Some kinda family reunion."

"I see. I think you may have lost something off your truck if you wouldn't mind stepping back there with me and taking a look."

"You mean get out?" The man's already red face deepened in color.

"Yes."

"Uh...well...you see," he began. His hands tightened on the steering wheel. "I..."

"It'll just take a few minutes." I stepped back and waited for him to climb down out of his rig, but he didn't. He just sat there staring at me. "Is there a problem, sir?" Silence and more staring. *Unbelievable!* "I'm going to need to see your driver's license."

The man removed his right hand from the steering wheel and reached for something in the seat. I placed my hand on my gun and stepped back and to the side a little more. When he offered his open wallet to me, I relaxed.

"Can you take it out for me, please?" I asked, moving back into position next to the driver side door.

"Oh, sure sure." He tugged on it a couple of times before it broke loose and he could remove it.

"Harold Swanson," I read. *Why does that name seem familiar?*

"Yes, ma'am." He grinned at me.

"Okay, Harold." I handed back his license. "We really need to check out your rig and make sure you don't have anything else that can come flying off and potentially cause a problem."

The grin disappeared. "I can't get out," he muttered.

"And why is that?"

"Well..." he began, "...you see I had an accident earlier."

"Are you injured?"

"No, nothing like that. It was my own fault, actually. In too big a hurry loading that john." He nodded toward the back of his truck. "I almost had it up on the platform when one of those crazy horses tried to bust outta the pen. Scared the bejeezus outta me and the damn thing slipped. Knocked me to the ground and slopped all over me!" He shook his head. "Didn't think those cowboys could've filled it that much."

Sucking my lips inward over my teeth, I looked down and to the left, fighting the urge to burst out laughing.

"Anyway, I managed to get it loaded onto the truck, but I was a mess. Had to use the hose to spray off my pants and boots, and then I hung them on the back of the truck to dry."

"Well, you've lost at least one boot," I said, "and I don't recall seeing anything flapping as I came up behind you."

"Oh man, you got to be kiddin' me," Harold said as he opened the door. A hairy leg with a dirty white sock on the end of it stretched down, searching for the truck step. With his back to me, he climbed out of his truck. When he turned around, he caught me staring at the bottom edge of his boxers hanging below the tails of his work shirt. They were made from red fabric with black and white hearts scattered across it. He looked from me to his underwear and shrugged. "My wife, Mabel, thinks it keeps our romance alive."

"I see," I said, nodding my head and again trying not to laugh. Then it came to me. I'd met Mabel Swanson the night before at the gas station, and this was *her* Harold.

The man carefully picked his way along the shoulder of the road in his stocking feet, trying to avoid the larger rocks. "Sonofabitch!" he exclaimed when he reached the back of his truck. "My boots were tied right there." He pointed to a hook at the back of the collection tank, above the coiled garden hose I assumed he used to spray himself off. "And my pants were hanging over here." He hobbled around to the other side of the truck. "Dammit, I don't see them anywhere."

Stepping closer to the truck, I spotted the missing boot amongst the green loops of hose. "Hey Harold," I called, "I found your other boot." I reached for it but decided that wasn't such a good idea. As he tip-toed back around the truck, I retrieved the other one from my patrol unit, making a mental note to rinse my hands off with one of my bottles of water.

When I got back to the sewage truck, Harold was sitting on the drop-down platform, next to the portable outhouse. He had pulled on one boot and was picking stickers out of the sock on his other foot.

"Can't tie this one, the lace is busted," he complained. I held up the other boot and the missing lace was still knotted to one of its laces. "Oh, there it is," he said, taking it from me and shoving his foot into it. "But I still ain't got no pants."

"Well..." I tried to focus on his sweat-drenched face and ignore his ridiculous outfit, but it was very difficult. "They're most likely along the side of the road somewhere."

He looked down and shook his head. "I hope so. I sure don't wanna have to explain this to Mabel, let along the guys at the water treatment plant when I go to dump my load." Then he tromped back to the cab and climbed in.

Feeling almost as sweaty as he looked, I returned to my own rig, turned around and headed home—again.

Chapter 9

It was just past eight Tuesday morning when I pulled into the parking lot on the west side of the Sheriff's Office. I grabbed the list of questions I'd printed off before leaving home and my personal radio, which I'd shoved into a plastic grocery bag, and went inside. "Hey Cindy," I said as I approached the dispatcher's desk.

She looked up from her stack of paperwork. "Oh hi, Sarah."

I leaned on the tall, circular counter that surrounded her desk on three sides. "I need to record some guys coming in to give statements. I assume we can do that, right?"

"Audio or video?"

"Just audio, but in both interrogation rooms."

"Hmm." She tapped her lips a few times with the end of her pen. "Check in the small cabinets in each room. I'm pretty sure there are video cameras inside but not sure about any other recording devices. If not there, check the storage room at the end of the hall. Or ask Josh. He might know."

"Okay. We still on for lunch?"

"You bet." Before we could discuss where, the phone rang, so I wandered around the corner to the interrogation rooms.

A quick search of each cabinet resulted in one small video camera and a tabletop tripod. *Time to go to the lab.* "How's my favorite lab tech?" I asked as I walked through the door.

"Just peachy," Josh said, "considering I'm the *only* lab tech. So whatcha got going on today?"

"Well, I brought you this." I held up the grocery bag.

He took it and peered inside. "Ah, the dead radio. Tell me again what you did to it."

"Dived in after a drowning victim."

"Wow, did you save them?"

I shook my head. "False alarm."

He frowned at me.

"It was a dummy in the water. Couple of kids pulling a prank."

"Holy cow." He sorted through the pile. "At least you pulled out the batteries, so it might be salvageable. It'll take me awhile to check it out, though."

"That's okay," I said. "I'll be here all morning, which brings me to my next problem. Do we have any way to make an audio recording?"

"I do it all the time, for taking notes." Josh put down the pieces of my radio he'd been inspecting and walked over to his desk. "I use the voice recorder on my tablet," he said, picking up the device and flipping back the cover. "That way I can make individual files for the different cases I'm working on."

"Do you think I could borrow that for a couple of hours? I have some interviews I want to record."

"Sure, and when you're done, we can save them to a flash drive for you."

"You don't by any chance have two of these, do you? Scott's going to be helping me, and I'd like to record his interviews, too."

Josh shook his head. "No, but I might still have the old junker cassette recorder I used before I got this." He laid the tablet back down on his desk and walked over to one of the tall metal cabinets that lined the back wall. After opening the doors, he dropped down to one knee and began pulling items off the bottom shelf. "Here it is," he said, holding up a large rectangular piece of ancient electronics. "Now all we need is a cassette." He placed the recorder on the large viewing table, where he'd dumped the remnants of my radio, and moved over to the myriad of drawers beneath the counter on the opposite wall. The first two tries were a bust but the third hit pay dirt. "Eureka!" he said, holding a small plastic case over his head. He grabbed the recorder, plugged the cord into the nearest outlet and popped in the cassette. "Test, test," he said, after pushing a couple of buttons. "One, two, three." A couple more clicks of the buttons and an electronic version of his voice repeated what he'd said. "There you are. Works perfect."

"Great! That one I think I can handle, but you better walk me through how to record on your tablet."

"Oh sure. You'll be surprised how easy it is."

A few minutes later, I walked out of the lab and headed for the interrogation rooms. I'd just gotten the equipment set up in each one when Scott showed up.

"So are we ready to do this thing?" he asked.

"Almost. I have the list of questions... " Or at least I did but had no idea where I'd left it. "Um, I'll get it for you in a second. Do you want to record the interviews on an electronic tablet or a cassette recorder?"

His crooked smile appeared. "Seeings how me and technology don't get along, I'll take the recorder."

"Okay. It's in the interrogation room closest to the entrance, and I'll get you that list of questions." *When I find it!*

Scott headed for the break room, and I returned to the lab. Josh was perched on a stool, his long legs intertwined with the rungs. "Hey, did I leave a piece of paper in here with a list of questions on it?"

When he looked up with googly eyes the size of silver dollars from the magnifying visor he had pulled down over his glasses, it took every bit of self-control I could muster not to laugh out loud. "Check over on that counter," he said, pointing with the tiny screwdriver he'd been using to probe the interior of my damaged radio.

I found what I was looking for, made a quick copy, and located Scott, who was still in the break room crunching on some corn nuts he'd gotten out of the vending machine. "Here you go," I said, handing him one of the sheets of paper. "Just have each interviewee state his name, address, and phone number at the beginning and then ask these questions."

"Seems simple enough," he said, glancing at the questions. "How many did you say there were?"

"Twenty, which is ten apiece."

"Hmm, ten interviews at about five minutes each." He squinted his eyes and made a couple of nods with his head. "That'll take about an hour, start to finish, give or take ten minutes. Better get another snack to tide me over 'til lunch," he said, dropping more coins into the vending machine.

Oh, brother! I shook my head. "Just be ready to go. They should be here any minute."

"Sure thing." He retrieved the package of cheese and crackers that he'd selected and tucked them into his pocket.

As I crossed the hall to the interrogation room I'd be using, a wave of wranglers surged through the front door. "Hey fellas," I called, traveling the short distance down the hall and past Cindy's desk. "Thanks for coming in." I scanned the faces under a sea of cowboy hats for Nate but didn't see him. "So, is everyone here?"

"Not quite," a voice said from the back of the group. "The guys driving the semi had to go aways down the road, looking for a place big enough to park in. And Nate said he had some business to tend to first, so he and Earl will be by later."

"I see. Okay then, we might as well get started. Do I have two volunteers?"

The men exchanged glances. "Do we get to leave as soon as we're done?" one of them asked.

"Of course."

"Then I'll go first," he said, "and so will Howie." He grabbed ahold of another wrangler's shirt front and pulled him along as he stepped forward. "He's driving." This got a roar of laughter from the others, and one of them clapped Howie on the back.

"This is Cindy," I said, sweeping my arm toward the dispatcher's desk, "and she can help you if you need anything."

A tall, skinny wrangler with a giant, black handlebar mustache stepped forward and removed his cowboy hat. "Well howdy, ma'am. It's a pleasure to meet you."

Cindy looked up from her paperwork just long enough to smile and return his greeting. I could hardly believe it. A few months ago, she would've been conducting her own interviews, getting contact information from any and all possible candidates. Being related to most of the available bachelors in the county had made dating challenging, to say the least. But since hooking up with Undersheriff Sandusky, she didn't seem to have more than a passing interest in the herd of cowboys loitering in the lobby. *What has Sandusky done to her?*

"You two follow me and we'll get started." I led them into the closest interrogation room and caught Scott pouring the last of the corn nuts into his mouth. "This is Deputy Jenkins," I said, glaring at him.

"Howdy," he sputtered, spraying chewed bits of his snack.

Without saying a word, I stepped over to the tape recorder and pressed the play and record button, followed by the pause button. "When you are ready to start, just press the pause button and count to ten. Then in between each interview you can hit pause again. If the tape runs out, just flip it over and record on that side." I turned toward the door. "Don't screw this up!" I warned, as I walked by him on the way out.

"No worries, I got this," he said, winking at me.

"Come on Howie," I said, "we'll step next door, and I'll have you out of here in no time."

It took a couple of tries before I got Josh's tablet into record mode, but once I figured it out, the interviews went smoothly as I asked each wrangler about where the group had gone after the roundup and what they had done. With very little variation, they all reported the same thing; no one had seen Ida after she drove away, they'd left the area around four o'clock and went to the Wagon Wheel Café for supper, after which they returned to the fairgrounds to unload and feed their horses. The rest of the evening was spent playing cards, reading, or making phone calls home. No one had been seen leaving other than Howie, who had driven Earl back out to the pens to spend the night.

Almost an hour later, I walked my eighth interviewee toward the entrance and was relieved to see Nate and Earl waiting in the lobby. "Glad to see you made it," I said.

"Yeah, sorry we're late," Nate said, "but there was something I had to take care of before heading this way."

"Nothing serious, I hope."

"Me too," he murmured.

"So, are we done here?" Scott asked as he escorted his own interviewee out.

"You're finished?"

"Yup. That was number ten."

"Well... " I looked at the two remaining men. "Can I get you to interview one of these guys, then they can be on their way?"

"Sure," he said, his crooked smile materializing, "but you'll owe me."

"Fine, I'll owe you."

Scott motioned to Nate. "Come on, let's see how fast we can do this."

"Suits me," Nate said, touching the brim of his hat as his eyes met mine. Then he followed Scott down the hallway.

"Come on, Earl," I said, leading the way.

"Yes, ma'am." He removed his hat and fell in behind me.

It was just before noon when I finished typing up the statements Scott and I had recorded, thanks to my competent typing skills. But, with only a few subtle differences, I actually could have copied and pasted their answers. It also became quite clear how Scott had finished so much faster than I had. He'd obviously handed each man the sheet of paper and had them read the questions to themselves and just told him the answers. I pictured him leaning back in his chair with his feet propped on top of the table, cramming cheese and crackers into his mouth. Not exactly standard procedure, but at least he got the job done.

I printed the transcript of the interviews and saved it to a flash drive along with the recording on Josh's tablet. Then I put them in a manila envelope and also dropped in the cassette tape out of the ancient recorder—just in case. Tucking it under my arm, I headed down the hall, hoping to find Sheriff Atkins in his office.

I knocked on the partially opened door and entered when granted permission. "Good morning, sir."

"Murdock."

"I was just checking to make sure you'd seen my request for a couple of days off next week."

"Seen it and approved."

I hesitated. "How about Scott? Did he get his request in yet?"

"Jenkins? Haven't seen it."

"Damn," I whispered.

"I take it he's going with you?"

"Yes, sir. Endurance ride."

He opened a side drawer of his desk, flipped through a few files and retrieved a familiar yellow piece of paper. "Fill in the top part and give it to dispatch, so they can adjust the shift schedule," he said, scribbling his signature at the bottom. "I'd rather have him with you than annoying me."

When I started as a deputy, almost a year ago, Scott prided himself on making fun of the fact Sheriff Atkins' mother had named him after the country-western singer, Chet Atkins. That is, until the sheriff caught him at it. Scott isn't at the top of the sheriff's shit list—that spot, I'm fairly certain, is held by Undersheriff Sandusky—but he's a close second.

"Thank you, sir." I took the paper he was holding and turned to leave.

"And Murdock?"

"Yes, sir."

"The next time you want company at a competition, try asking someone who takes it seriously."

"You?"

He nodded. "Marshall and I... " he began, pointing to the photograph of a buckskin horse, hanging behind his desk, "... took first place at the Virginia City 100 mile ride last month."

"That's very impressive; I had no idea. Raven and I typically compete in shorter rides but I've always wanted to try a longer one."

"Well, perhaps next year we both can compete."

"Yes sir, I'd like that."

He stared at me for a few seconds. "Was there anything else?"

"Oh, no sir." I turned toward the door and suddenly remembered I did have one more thing to ask. "Actually," I said, turning back to face him. "I need to get Raven shod. Is there a good farrier around?"

"Ed Flowers, over at the High Desert Hot Springs," he said without looking up. "Best one in the county."

Ed? "Okay, great. Thanks." I stepped through the doorway and returned the door to its partially opened position before walking back up the hallway. As I rounded the corner, a fellow officer radioed into dispatch.

"Modoc, 125 requesting a radio check."

"Copy 125, you're 10-1."

"That Scott?" I asked Cindy as I approached the high counter.

"Yeah, he had to head for Tulelake to patrol."

"Oh fun. Somebody sick?"

Cindy shook her head. "Joe had to take his mom to the doctor in Redding." She reached under her desk and grabbed her purse. "My uncle and aunt have to make that drive a couple times a month, and it takes all day. Medford is closer, but insurance doesn't always cross state lines." She came out from behind her desk and started for the front door. "Come on, I'm starving."

"So, where do you want to go?"

"The new market out on 299. They make killer sandwiches." As we pushed through the front door, I hoped that was a good thing.

Before returning to Surprise Valley, I stopped by the office to see if my radio was salvageable and to ask Josh about Ida's car. I found him in the break room munching on a peanut butter and jelly sandwich. "Hey, any luck with my radio?" I asked, pulling out a chair at his table and sitting down.

He chewed a few more times and swallowed before answering. "Yeah, it's on my desk and ready to go."

"Great, thanks. And how about the Nissan? Find anything useful?"

"It's on my to-do list but you kinda been monopolizing my time this morning."

"Oh yeah, I suppose I have." I grinned at him. "Sorry about that, but if you find anything that might help me figure out what happened to her, let me know."

"Will do," he said just before taking another big bite of his sandwich. With nothing more to discuss, I grabbed my radio on the way out and headed for Cedar Pass.

Chapter 10

"Come on, Raven. Just a few more laps," I said, clucking my tongue and snapping the whip a couple of times. The large, black horse snorted and shook his head. "Quit your complaining. I still have to do my own workout."

He slowed to a walk despite my best effort to keep him moving. That is until Bubbles trotted between his feet. Then he blew up, kicking out his back legs and tossing his head so much, you would've thought he was a bucking bronco at the rodeo. Struggling to hold onto the lunge line, he dragged me around a bit before I managed to get him calmed down enough to pull off his halter. As soon as Raven realized he was free, he tore off toward the end of the field and trotted back and forth along the fence, his mane and tail fluttering behind him.

"Well Bubbles, that was one way to get him moving but not exactly what I had in mind," I told the miniature mutt as I put away the equipment I'd been using. "Now it's my turn, so you better find some way to occupy yourself until I'm done." On the way back to the house, I stepped into the bathhouse and quickly sprayed down the rock-lined sides of my hot tub. Turning on the hose to a slow trickle, the temperature of the water coming out of the natural hot springs was cooler than usual, and the tub would be just about filled by the time I finished my workout.

Appreciative of the slightly cooler weather the last couple of days, I was still hot and sweaty when I reached the house. I pulled off my dusty tennis shoes and exchanged the old pair of jeans I'd put on after work for some shorts. I hauled the oscillating fan from my room into the spare bedroom where I'd been meeting regularly with my sparring dummy.

I was just about to run through my routine of Tae Kwon Do moves when I suddenly realized I hadn't called Ed Flowers about shoeing Raven. Returning to my bedroom, I fished my phone out of the pocket of the discarded jeans and searched through my contacts. Not finding a number for the resort, I stepped out to the sunroom, a.k.a my office, and located the number in an old phone book I'd found when I moved in. My call was answered after a couple of rings.

"High Desert Hot Springs. How may I help you?"

"Mrs. Flowers?"

"Yes?"

"Hi, it's Sarah Murdock."

"Oh hello, dear. How are you?"

I was surprised she remembered me but was glad she did. "I'm fine, thank you. I was hoping to speak to your husband. Is he there, by chance?"

"Why, yes he is." A loud clunk, footsteps and then, "Ed! Phone!" she called, obviously several feet from the receiver. After a brief moment of silence, she came back on the line. "He'll be right here, dear."

"Thank you, Mrs. Flowers."

"Oh please, call me Abigail."

"Yes, ma'am."

"So tell me, are you working on any interesting cases these days?"

Before I could answer, there was a click followed by, "Hello?"

"Hi Ed, it's Sarah Murdock."

"Who?"

"You know, that wonderful deputy that helped our Tom," Abigail interjected.

"Oh... yes," he replied. "Uh, how can I help you?"

"I was hoping you'd have time this Saturday to shoe my horse."

"Well... "

"I have your calendar right here," Abigail interjected again, "and it looks like you have something in the afternoon, but your morning is wide open."

The man let out a huge sigh. "Thank you, Abby." The image of him slouched in his lawn chair on the shore of Sworinger Reservoir popped into my head.

"Welcome. Good-bye, Sarah." And she hung up.

"Are you sure Saturday will work for you?" I asked.

"Don't see why not. It'll get me outta the house for a couple of hours. Around nine o'clock be all right?"

"Yeah, that should be fine. I'll have Raven haltered and ready to go."

"Great. Now, where do you live?"

I gave him directions to my place, hung up, and returned to my workout in the spare bedroom, where I found Bubbles curled up on the hide-a-bed sofa, waiting.

I dropped one of my favorite CDs into my portable stereo, hit play and cranked the volume.

As I warmed up, I tried to focus on my breathing and technique, but I couldn't get the missing protestor out of my head. *What has happened to her? Is she still alive?*

"Concentrate!" I told myself as I began my upper body routine. "Uppercut, left hook, elbow jab," I chanted over and over, making contact with the higher paddles on my sparring dummy and increasing my speed each time until I was panting, and beads of sweat began to form on my face. Finally in the zone, I switched to side and front kicks, completing several sets on each leg and finished up trying to perfect my crescent and roundhouse kicks. By the time I was done, my muscles were spent, and I was drenched.

After snagging my robe of its hook on the back of the bathroom door, I jerked open the door of the fridge, intending to grab a couple of beers, but it was like my body took over, and my hand closed around a bottle of water instead. "Come on Dog," I said, heading for the front door. "Time to relax."

The water, having almost reached the top of the hot tub, looked so inviting that I tossed my robe onto the small bench, stripped off my clothes and jumped in, sending a miniature tsunami over the edge. An instant later, I was joined by Bubbles, who happily paddled around me as I stretched out and floated weightlessly in the crystal-clear water.

As the tension left my muscles and I began to relax, my thoughts tumbled like dominoes—horse riding to wild horses to roundups to wranglers to protestors. Suddenly Ida Dudley popped into my brain. *Dammit!* No matter what I tried to think of instead, she wormed her way back in until I was so utterly frustrated, I submerged myself. When I finally ran out of air, I burst through the surface of the water, took some deep breaths, and decided to analyze the facts as I knew them.

Ida showed up at the roundup and, after creating a scene, drove off. None of the wranglers reported seeing her after she left. Her car was found at the gas station being filled with gasoline, but there was no sign of her. A neighbor saw her car pull in... *Had she seen Ida?* I didn't know. *Did she see Ida after the truck and trailer pulled out?* I didn't know that either. And where had Ida been between the time she left the roundup and when she pulled into the gas station? *Was she even the one that pulled her car into the gas station?* I had no way of knowing that either. *Does the gas station have surveillance cameras outside?* I hadn't bothered to ask Mike about that.

"Well, I guess that settles it," I told Bubbles as he climbed out of the tub and shook himself off. "I need to go back to Rabbit Traxx and do some follow-up investigating. Seems I have some questions that need answering. And," I added, lying back again and staring at the ceiling, "perhaps someone will recognize her when her picture comes out in the paper and remember seeing her somewhere." Satisfied that I had a plan, I stayed in the hot tub until Bubbles whined and scratched at the door, and I was as wrinkled as a prune.

As I waited for Mike to pull up the footage from the previous Sunday on the surveillance tape at Rabbit Traxx, I walked along the edge of the parking lot closest to where Ida's car had been found, looking for anything out of the ordinary among the small bushes and grass that grew there. A cast-off beer can, a discarded candy wrapper, and a dirty old sock provided no viable clues, so I meandered over to the east side of the building, turned around and studied the far row of pumps, again speculating whether or not it had actually been Ida driving her car that night, and if so, how quickly could someone grab her and shove her inside—and where. "I wonder if Mabel saw the door of that livestock trailer open."

"Nope."

Astonished to receive an answer in such close proximity, I spun around and crouched into a defensive position with my arms in front of me and ready to punch the assailant, who happened to be the very person I was thinking about.

"Whoa there," Mabel said, backing up a few steps.

"Sorry." I lowered my arms and straighten up, as heat rose from my neck to my forehead. The embarrassing moment reminded me of a sneak attack by a wild turkey while visiting my parents last Christmas—but that's a different story.

"Well, I saw you wandering around out here and thought I'd come see what you're doing." She looked around before leaning in closer and whispering, "Does it have something to do with that wild-looking woman that's gone missing?"

"So, you must have seen her picture in the paper this morning."

"Sure did."

"That was her car I was asking you about last Sunday." I

retrieved my notebook in case she had information I could use. "Did you happen to see her get out of her vehicle after she pulled in?" I asked, pulling a pen from my shirt pocket.

"To be honest, I did see some kind of movement, but I had my readers on and couldn't really make out what was happening. I'd just gotten my new copy of BHG and was enjoying it while Harold watched his program."

"BHG?"

"*Better Homes and Gardens.* I just love their home improvement and gardening articles."

"Which way was the car facing when it pulled in?"

"That way," she said, pointing towards the Warner Mountains on our left.

"And the truck and livestock trailer? Did it pull in behind the car?"

"No. It was on this side of the pumps and facing the other way."

"I see," I said, jotting down some notes. "And did you see anything while the truck was there?"

Mable frowned, as if trying to remember. "Let me see. The brake lights went on a couple of times, I think, but that's it."

"So you didn't see the door at the back of the trailer open?"

She shook her head. "I had my readers off by then, and if I squint, most things come into focus."

"After the truck pulled out, did you see anyone around?"

Again, she shook her head. "About then a commercial came on, and Harold hollered for another beer. I didn't see anything else going on until you showed up."

"Well, maybe there will be something on the surveillance tape," I said, returning my notebook and pen to their respective pockets. "Thanks again for your help."

As Mabel made her way back across the street to her house, I pulled open the front door of the little store inside the gas station and stepped through. "Any luck with that tape, Mike?"

"I found the stuff from Sunday but you really can't see much," the attendant said. "Here, I'll rewind it and you can take a look for yourself."

I moved around to the other side of the glass counter and stood next to Mike. The picture on the tiny monitor was not the best, and the angle of the camera gave a clear view of the area between the front door and the closest row of gas pumps. However, the far side of the second row was out of view, so the camera never captured Ida pulling in and only the lower half of the truck and livestock trailer. Even after watching the video three times, I saw no indication that the backdoor of the trailer had been opened, and the time stamp on the video indicated that the vehicle was there a mere five minutes before pulling out again. I thanked Mike for allowing me to look at it and left.

The only remaining possibility for any clues to Ida's disappearance was her car. I grabbed my cell phone and dialed the office. Less than a minute later, the young lab technician came on the line. "Hey Josh, it's Sarah. I was just wondering what you'd found in that Nissan that got brought in."

"Well, nothing too exciting. I filled two garbage bags with trash, mostly from food purchases. Any receipts I came across are in an evidence bag. Her purse, wallet and cell phone are all catalogued. The clothes from the trunk filled another garbage bag, and there was a digital camera in a carrying case with a SD card with pictures of horses in some kind of pens."

"Okay, thanks. Can you transfer me back to Cindy?"

"Sure thing. Hold on."

"Dispatch."

"Hi Cindy, it's me. Have we gotten any calls on that missing person yet?"

"Nope, nothing. I'll let you know as soon as we do, though."

"Thanks. Talk to you later." I snapped my phone shut and shoved it back into my pocket. I considered contacting Carol Gann to see if she had heard from Ida, assuming Lulu had gotten her contact information. However, since Ida's phone was in her car, that most likely had not happened. Completely frustrated with the investigation, if you could even call it that, I decided a late breakfast was warranted.

"Well hello, Hon. You're just the person I was gonna call when I went on break," Sal called out to me when I entered the Wagon Wheel Café a few minutes later.

"Why is that?" I asked, settling into my favorite spot at the counter. I tugged a menu free from its holder and began scanning the choices.

The geriatric waitress grabbed the coffee pot and what looked like a section of newspaper before heading my way. "This here." She plopped the paper down in front of me. It had been folded to reveal the photograph of Ida Dudley, in living color. The messy halo of reddish hair provided the perfect background for the wide-eye glare and satanic leer captured by the camera operated by the Colorado Division of Motor Vehicles. "I seen her the other day," she said, jabbing the paper a few times with her index finger.

My heart seemed to skip a beat. "You did? Where?"

"Why right here at this very counter." She snagged a cup, placed it in front of me and began filling it with the strong, restaurant coffee.

"And when did you see her?" I asked trying to control the emotion in my voice.

"Last Sunday. She came in just before our regular church-goers arrived. So that'd be just before noon. She ordered an egg salad sandwich and a Coke."

My excitement fizzled like a lit match being squeezed between wet fingertips. *At least now I know where she went right after she left the roundup.* "But you haven't seen her since then?"

"Nope, just that one time." She pulled her pad out of her apron pocket and her pen out of the pile of platinum hair on top of her head. "What'll ya have?" She leaned in a little closer. "Cookie got a good do on the gravy this morning."

Technically, I was in training, but one order of fluffy, soft biscuits covered in creamy, country gravy wouldn't... "I'll have a veggie omelet, no hash browns, and dry wheat toast." *Who said that?*

Sal shook her head as she jotted down my order. Then she tore the page off her pad and snapped it onto the circular ticket holder that hung over the pass-through window into the kitchen before retrieving a freshly brewed carafe of coffee and making the rounds.

I can't seem to catch a break with a butterfly net! No viable clues and no witnesses to Ida's disappearance left me absolutely nothing to go on. The woman had just vanished. Staring at her picture in the newspaper, I hoped that someone somewhere had seen her and would contact the Sheriff's Office. Until that happened, I decided to do my job and focus on my upcoming competition, hoping the woman wasn't dead or lay dying in the middle of nowhere.

Chapter 11

By eight-thirty Saturday morning, the thermometer hanging on the side of the small shed that doubled as a tack room registered move than ninety degrees. "Well Raven," I said, prying the last of the compacted dirt from his right front hoof, "looks like our reprieve from the miserably hot weather is over." He moved his massive head up and down in agreement.

I'd just finished brushing him, trying to relax him as much as possible, when a familiar dark grey GMC pickup glided down the short hill between my place and Remy's. Towing a small, silver trailer that resembled a supersized hot dog stand, it pulled into my driveway, made a loop in front of the bathhouse, and backed through the open gate into Raven's field. I recognized Ed Flowers the moment he climbed out, but it took a second or two to realize his passenger was Tom Lowry.

I'd first met Tom several months ago during a murder investigation where, at one point, he was implicated as a suspect. But after hearing the confession of the actual murderer, I realized his only crime was associating himself with the wrong people and being in the wrong place at the wrong time. "Good morning Ed," I said, walking toward the men.

"Morning Deputy," he replied.

"Please, call me Sarah. And how are things with you, Tom?"

He smiled. "Couldn't be better. Made some money selling my rabbits, and me and Ed have been pretty busy this summer what with all the horses we've had to shoe and projects at the resort." The man of mixed heritage did not display any of the anger I'd seen the first time I met him. Instead, he seemed much more accepting of who he was and where he'd come from.

"Fine looking animal you got there," Ed said, walking toward Raven. The gelding's nostrils flared as the man offered his hand before making his way around the large animal, feeling down each leg as he went. "How is he with people working on his feet?"

A tug of war over a hind hoof between Scott and Raz the Spaz came to mind. "Better than most," I replied. "Although he does have his moments."

"Fair enough." He looked back toward his rig. "We about ready to go, Tom."

"Almost. Just have to hook up the forge." While Ed and I had been talking, Tom had unlatched the sides of the supersized hot dog cart and lifted them up. The panels, held in place by hydraulic supports, provided a makeshift roof for the miniature blacksmith's workshop.

"Wow, this is quite the set-up," I said, walking over to check it out. "Did you build this?"

Ed chuckled. "No, it's an actual manufactured farrier's trailer that I've outfitted with my own equipment."

Constructed entirely of stainless steel, the passenger side had an enormous rack that held horse shoes of every style and size. A tower of drawers sat behind that, and an anvil and what I assumed was the forge Tom had mentioned were attached to arms that extended out the back. A grinder, drill press, and small generator took up the remainder of the workbench on the driver's side. Tom had also removed two small roll-around carts and was filling them with a variety of tools Ed would need during the shoeing.

"Might as well get started." Ed grabbed the handle of one of the carts and carried it back to where Raven was dozing in the sunshine. The clank of it being set down next to him didn't seem to bother him, so I was hopeful. Because I'd boarded him in a stable back in Virginia and they usually arranged for the farrier, I had no idea how he actually behaved; I only knew he didn't seem to mind when I cleaned his hooves with the pick and had been was fairly tolerant when Scott trimmed them.

"So it looks like he had shoes on a while ago," Ed said after raising one of the horse's hooves and straddling it for inspection.

"That's right. They were put on last February, just before I moved him out here. A buddy of mine pulled them off in April, trimmed his hooves, and then trimmed them again at the end of June."

"Uh-huh," he said but made no other comment until he had inspected the other three. "So they don't look too bad. Why are you wanting to put shoes back on him now?"

"I've entered an endurance competition and want to protect his feet from possible rocky terrain."

"Well, then... " He walked around Raven again. "I think I'm going to change the angle just a bit to give him a little more support to his legs and prevent muscle fatigue."

"Sounds good to me," I said. *At this point, I'll take any advantage I can get.*

"Tom, bring that piece of plywood over here," Ed called as he scooted the cart closer with the toe of his boot and picked up Raven's hoof again. Using a curved knife, he scraped off the outer layer, switched tools, and trimmed off what looked like a giant black toe nail. Then he grabbed a large rasp and filed the hoof until the surface was smooth. Just before he released it, Tom slid the small, square board into position. "Yeah, that looks about right," Ed said, after studying the hoof for a moment. He quickly repeated the procedure on the remaining three hooves, Tom moving the flat wooden surface for him each time.

"Now, let's select a shoe," Ed said, moving around to the passenger side of the trailer. "I'm thinking maybe a size one."

"Two," Tom said.

"No, I'm fairly certain he'll need a one." Ed selected the shoe he wanted, and I followed him back over to Raven. He picked up the front foot again and held the shoe in place. After looking it over for several seconds, he released the foot and straightened up. Before he could say anything, Tom offered the horse shoe he had in his hand.

"Two."

There was a brief moment of silent communication between the two of them. "Yes, size two," Ed agreed as he traded shoes with Tom. "Light us up and get the other three lined out."

While Tom got the forge going and filled a small bucket with water, Ed took each shoe in turn and checked it against its prospective hoof, mumbling to himself the entire time. Finally, he went back to the first one and slid it inside the forge. As it heated up, he carried the second roll-around cart over to where Raven was still patiently waiting.

"So, when is this competition of yours?" he asked, returning to the trailer to check on the heating shoe.

"Next weekend. I've been doing some training in the Hays Canyon Range near the end of Highway 299. It's good for hill work, but I'd really like to find a place not quite as steep and without fences to contend with, where I can ride out cross-country for two or three hours and work on our pacing."

"Need to come farther north," Tom said. He was leaning against the workbench with his arms crossed over his chest. "No fences for at least fifteen miles."

"Really?" I asked. "How far north?"

"Maybe start at Fee Reservoir or Big Mud Lake and head east into Nevada. Nothing too steep until you drop down to Mosquito Lake as long as you stay on top of the ridge at Three Canyons."

"Three Canyons?"

"It's where three canyons come together but there's a way through in the center."

More familiar with the reservoir, I at least knew of a place to maneuver and park the horse trailer. It sounded promising, and I was anxious to check it out on the map hanging on the wall of my office.

Ed pulled the glowing horse shoe out of the forge and

began customizing the shape. By the time he was satisfied, it had returned to its original color but still had to be extremely hot.

Continuing to doze, the gelding didn't pay much attention when his hoof left the ground. However, when Ed placed the shoe against it and tendrils of smoke went up Raven's nose, he jerked against the tied lead rope and shifted his weight toward the man holding his foot. Not that I could blame him; it kind of freaked me out as well.

"Tom," Ed called, struggling to hold the shoe in place, "a little help here."

Before I could react, the man reached the animal's head in four long strides, tugging something from his back pocket as he went. Retrieving a handkerchief similar to the ones I'd seen Remy use, he grabbed the gelding's halter and held the cloth up to his black, velvety nose.

The lead rope went slack as Raven leaned toward Tom. Barely moving the kerchief from the animal's nose, he shook it out, folded it into a triangle and tied it loosely around both nostrils, creating a comical equine outlaw.

I moved in next to him. "How did you do that?"

He leaned back against the hitching post, "Old Indian trick," he said. My raised eyebrow and tilted head apparently conveyed my disbelief because he chuckled after a few seconds. "Okay, I confess," he said, raising both hands in the air. "Essential oils."

"What?"

"There's lavender oil on the hanky. Has a very calming effect on dogs and horses."

"I'll say it does. I've never seen Raven calm down like

that." I patted his massive neck. "Maybe I should get myself some."

Before we could discuss the miracle of essential oils any further, Ed returned with the horse shoe he'd just cooled down in the bucket of water and began nailing it to Raven's hoof. "I usually just use four nails," he said as he made the last couple of strikes with his hammer, seating the first one in place and twisting off the excess with the claw. "But I'm gonna put three on each side. Don't want your horse throwing a shoe during your ride."

"I appreciate that."

Acknowledging that the men had everything under control, I sneaked to the house to plot out my potential route. I easily located Fee Reservoir on my map and, sliding my finger east, Mosquito Lake. Backtracking, I found the place Tom was talking about and saw that I could bypass all three canyons by sticking to the ridge he'd mentioned. Looking at the reservoir again and the roads surrounding it, I figured the best place to park would be at its northern tip where County Road 212 connects with Fee Reservoir Road. From there, Raven and I should have a straight run to the east.

As I stepped into the kitchen to get some water, a soft thud came from the bedroom, followed by the clicking of toenails on linoleum. "Well, hello Dog. Been sleeping on my bed again?" I asked the miniature mutt.

Bubbles shook himself, sat down in the middle of the floor, and stared at me.

"What? You've already had breakfast and your water bowl is full."

The small dog continued to look at me.

"And you aren't coming outside either." I grabbed three bottles of water out of the fridge. "Don't need you out there getting Raven all riled up," I added, "so go lie down somewhere, and when they're all done, maybe we'll go for a ride."

That seemed to satisfy the small dog because he trotted into the living room and stretched out on the couch. Shaking my head, I went back outside.

Things must have continued to go well because Ed was finishing up the last shoe when I walked up. Raven, with his bandana still in place, was doing his best to ignore the whole process. "Okay, Tom. Walk him around a bit and let me get a good look at them," Ed said as he released the last hoof and pulled the carts of tools out of the way.

Tom removed the handkerchief with one hand while he untied the lead rope with the other. As he led the gelding around in a large circle, Raven shook his head a couple of times and his eyelids fluttered as if he was coming out of a drunken stupor.

"Looks good," Ed said, after studying the horse's feet for a few minutes. "Go ahead and turn him loose."

The moment the lead rope was unhooked, my horse shifted his weight toward his rump, spun to the left, and took off for the far side of his pasture at a dead run. "He sure likes his freedom," Tom said, rolling up the rope and handing it to me.

"Yes, he does."

As I flashed on the two times he'd gotten away from me, both of which would've left me stranded in the middle of nowhere if it hadn't been for the good Samaritans that rescued me, the two men began closing down the portable blacksmith's workshop. Within ten minutes, they were ready to go, so I paid Ed and bid both of them good-bye. Then I headed for the house to collect the dog and grab my keys.

Not wanting to block the road, I parked my Dooley next to the Applegate-Lassen Trail marker at the summit of Fandango Pass and walked back down the road until the northern part of Surprise Valley came into view. Scanning the east edge through my binoculars, I located Fee Reservoir and followed the slope up to an enormous high plateau just south of the highest peak in that stretch of the range.

"I'll need lots of water, some snacks, and of course, my GPS," I told my traveling companion, who ignored me as he explored along the road under the guardrail. "It should be a great ride. I just wish it were cooler so you could tag along."

Even though a slight breeze moved through the trees at the higher altitude, the heat was stifling and unless the temperature was significantly cooler tomorrow, I would have to be careful.

Chapter 12

Raven's body quivered as I made a final adjustment to the cinch strap on my endurance saddle. "You seem as excited as I am about this ride." The gelding tossed his head up and down several times. "I just hope it's an uneventful one," I added as I secured the nylon saddlebags in place. I'd balanced the weight, dividing my water—three bottles on each side—and stowing protein bars in one and apples in the other. Having learned a valuable lesson, however, I did not drop my keys into either side. Instead, I zipped them inside a small fanny pack I'd rummaged from the back of my closet along with an extra bottle of water, my GPS and my cell phone. After making sure the truck and trailer were secure, I tightened the strap on my camo bush hat and swung myself onto Raven's back.

I held him to a walk until we reached the gentle rise to the first plateau. Then I leaned forward slightly and gave the horse his head. Our pace quickened as he approached his competitive gait, but by the time we reached the top where the landscape leveled out, he was blowing hard, and his neck was wet with sweat even though I'd checked his pace several times. "Take it easy, Big Fella," I said, walking him in a large circle a couple of times. "It's too hot to be going balls out today."

When his breathing became less labored, we continued our ride toward the next rise. Starting up the slope, I again gave him his head, anxious to see if he would do a better job self-regulating his pace. We'd just made it about halfway to the top when he suddenly squatted down on his haunches like a trained cutting horse with his head up and ears forward, practically launching me out of the saddle. "What the hell, Raven!" I scolded when I got my composure back. His body tensed again and his head swung to the left. Looking in the same direction, I spotted what had his full attention.

A small band of wild horses had gathered at a natural spring. Surrounded by lush green vegetation, the force of the water had displaced a section of earth, forming a small pool. "Oh no you don't." I tightened my grip on the reins. "No adventure today." I nudged his sides with my knees until he finally continued to climb.

After twenty minutes riding straight for the rising sun, we approached a high ridge connecting three deep canyons. I slowed Raven to a walk and studied the terrain, making note of any unusual landmarks. Visualizing the map on my wall, I recalled that Three Canyons was about a third of the way to Mosquito Lake, and it had taken us about thirty minutes to get that far. If we continued for another hour, we'd have traveled around ten miles—a good distance for a practice run. I checked my watch. After a rest of forty-five minutes or so, we'd be back to Fee Reservoir around noon. *And I'll be floating in my tub before two.* Pleased with my plan, I urged the gelding on.

Soon we were making our way up the next slope, navigating around the occasional outcropping of volcanic rock. Adjusting our speed to the terrain, we trekked up one hill and down the next until we reached the base of the tallest peak. A small patch of shade created by a lone juniper tree provided a good spot to rest, so I dismounted and dug out some water. Two bottles went into a collapsible bucket for Raven, and I chugged down most of another one before pulling off my hat and pouring the rest of it over my head. Refreshed, I retrieved a granola bar for myself and an apple for my mount and crouched on the only rock in the shade.

Wanting to stretch my legs before heading back, I decided to lead Raven up the hill and check out what was on the other side. Part way up, I spotted a few buzzards circling in the distance. The higher I climbed, more and more birds stacked in a slowly spinning spiral became visible. I stopped counting at twenty.

Cresting the top of the hill, I discovered a seemingly endless valley and was surprised to find a small complex of buildings and corrals at the bottom of the extremely steep decline. A light breeze carried the rancid smell of dead animal, and a faint metallic clanking sound drifted up from an old windmill. As I scanned the surrounding area for the carrion, I spotted something that seemed out of place but couldn't really tell what it was. Going straight down the hill was too treacherous, so I looked around for an alternate route and located a game trail off to the right. Climbing back on my horse, I started down. Wider than most, I speculated it was a path frequently used by wild horses living in the area.

Several minutes later, we'd reached the valley floor and were on the way to investigate. About forty feet away, I realized it was a human body lying face up a few feet from one of the corrals. I dismounted and adjusted the reins so they hung down from Raven's bit to the ground, which is his signal to stay put. Within a few steps, I could see the body was that of a female—and one I'd seen before. "Oh shit," I whispered as I crept toward it.

Scanning the body for signs of life, I did not detect any movement at all. I knelt by the missing protestor's head and was reaching out to check for a pulse when the torso twitched, and the body jerked into a sitting position, a piercing scream shattering the silence. I tumbled backward and landed on my tailbone hard enough to make my teeth chatter.

"Why are you screaming?" I demanded, scrambling to my feet and dusting myself off.

"Who... " She spun around onto her hands and knees. "Oh—hey, I know you. I thought you were a buzzard!"

"What are you talking about?" I asked, stepping forward and offering her a hand.

She ignored my gesture and struggled to her feet. "I was trying to lure in one of them by playing dead," she said pointing to the column of scavengers still circling over our heads.

"And why would you do that?"

The woman stared at me as if my question was the most stupid one ever uttered. "So I could eat it, of course."

"Oh," I said, barely nodding my head. "Of course."

It had been a week since I'd seen Ida Dudley, but in that time her appearance had changed drastically. Her hair, no longer pulled back into a bun, was greasy and hung around her dirt-streaked, sunburned face. The center part was a wide, grey stripe across the top of her head, and her sunken cheeks made her look even more horse-like. Her clothes were torn in a few places and caked with dried mud. The oddest thing was her footwear. Two large socks, which came up to her knees, had been pulled on over her jeans, and they had an odd rectangular shape on the bottom.

"How did you get here?" I asked.

"I walked."

"Walked? From Cedarville?"

Again she gave me that stupid question look. "No! From over there," she said, pointing toward a small nob to the south.

"And how did you get over there?" I could feel my patience wearing thin.

"Well, obviously someone left me there."

I took a deep breath. "Why don't you start from the beginning. What's the last thing you remember before being left out here?"

"I was getting gas in town when someone pulled a bag over my head and threw me inside some kind of trailer, I think. I tried screaming for help and banging on the side, but whoever it was gave me a shot or something because the next thing I knew I was waking up in some old house."

"Did you get a look at who grabbed you?"

"No, too dark and too fast. And whoever it was took my shoes and socks, so I had to make some." She held up one foot for me to look at. "But there wasn't any water or food—oh, that reminds me—do have anything to eat? I'm starving!"

"Oh, yeah. Hang on a second." I walked over to where Raven was still patiently waiting and grabbed a protein bar and an apple out of my saddlebags. Looping my arm through his reins, I went back and offered them to Ida.

"Thanks," she said, snatching both items out of my hands. She devoured the apple, including the core, like Mr. Peepers, the monkey boy. Then she tore the wrapper off the bar and gobbled it down, too. "Mmm, that was good!" She swiped her mouth with the upper part of her left sleeve. "Got any more?"

I retrieved the rest of my rations and handed them over. "When's the last time you had anything to eat?"

"Let me see." She bit off a huge chunk of the protein bar. "I haven't had anything to eat since I polished off the Spam... was that yesterday... no at least two days ago," she said around a mouthful of goo. "What day is it, anyway?"

"Sunday."

"Sunday?" She forcibly swallowed the contents of her mouth. "I've been here for a week?"

I nodded. "Do you need some water?"

"That I have all I want." She pointed to the windmill that continued to make a clanking sound as it slowly spun around. "Good thing I know how they work so I could get that one going. The water is almost clear but still tastes kinda funny."

"How did you find this place?"

"Like I said, there wasn't any food or water there, so I walked one direction and then another until I found this place. That building over there," she said, pointing to the smaller one behind us, "has a kitchen. All I found was a box of macaroni and cheese and a can of Spam. I gathered some wood and built a fire in the little wood stove inside, but it was taking the water too long to boil, so I just dumped in the macaroni and let it soak for a while so it wasn't crunchy. I was so hungry I ate all of it, but I managed to stretch the Spam out for a couple of days.

"I tried to walk to the top of that hill but these... " She again lifted up one of her feet to show me. "... only work on flat ground, so I was pretty much stuck here. How did you find me, anyway?"

"Uh, well... " I didn't want to tell her it had been purely accidental that I found her but saw no other alternative. "Actually, I had no idea you were here. There were no clues as to what happened to you. It was as if you'd vanished. I just happened to be riding out here and spotted you from up there," I said, pointing toward the top of the steep incline. "But, I'll make a phone call and get help on its way." I pulled out my cell phone and flipped it open. "Damn!"

"What is it?" Ida asked.

"No service. I'll have to ride up to the top of the hill and see if that helps."

"What if it doesn't?" The pitch of her voice increased. "What then?"

"Well, then we'll keep going until my phone has service," I said, closing it and slipping it back into my fanny pack.

"But, I told you I can only walk on flat ground with these." She held up one of her feet for the third time. "How am I going to get up there?"

That's when I realized her *we* and my *we* were entirely different. "I meant my horse and me, not you."

"What do you mean 'not you'?" she bellowed as she began pacing back and forth and flailing her arms. "You can't leave me here—out in the middle of nowhere with nothing to eat!"

"Look," I began, "I don't know how far I will have to go before I can call for help." Trying to maintain eye contact, my head turned from side to side like I was watching a tennis match. Finally, I reached out and caught her by both shoulders. "I'm not sure my horse will ride double, and it's too far to go if he did." I released her and stepped back. "It will take me about an hour and a half to get back to my truck. I'm pretty sure I'll have service there, if not sooner. As soon as I do, I'll call for help, and someone will come get you."

"Someone? You just told me you had no idea where I was! How are they going to find me?" she shrieked.

"Ida, calm down. I can tell them where you are." I pulled my GPS out of the fanny pack. "I will just drop a marker here at our location. See?" I held it up for her to look at. "That way they will know right where you are."

Again, the how-can-you-be-so-stupid look. "And how are they going to get that little device of yours?" she asked, crossing her arms in front of her.

I opened my mouth to say something and then closed it again. *Dammit, she's right!* Only focusing on getting somewhere that would allow me to make a phone call and how long that would take, I hadn't even given any consideration as to how much time it would take to reach this location or what would be the best way to do so. There were only two possibilities—vehicle or helicopter. Obviously a helicopter would get here faster, but then there was the question of whether or not one was available. The situation didn't really call for an air ambulance, so what other options were there. I thought maybe the BLM or Forest Service might have one but how far away were they? I didn't even remember seeing one at the Cedarville Airport but that didn't mean a rancher didn't have one tucked away somewhere. I figured Cindy might know who had one, but it was Sunday and Ira Fielding was the dispatcher on duty, and well... sometimes I wondered if Ira even knew what planet he was on. And even if I located a helicopter to fly out here, how familiar with this part of Nevada might the pilot be? It truly was out in the middle of nowhere. That's when I realized I had no choice. "Okay," I conceded, "I'll come back to get you."

No service. Not surprised, I snapped my phone shut and secured it in my fanny pack before looking down at the woman waiting at the base of the steep slope. "No good!" I shouted down to her. "I'll need to head back, but as soon as I can, I'll call for help."

"Wait!" she screamed. "I changed my mind. Don't leave me here!"

Spinning Raven to the left and away from the edge, I waved to Ida, who continued to jump up and down and scream at me. I'd used my best powers of persuasion to convince her that traveling on my own was the best option. That, and a quick getaway while she was distracted for a brief moment, allowed me to get on my horse and ride back up the trail to the top of the peak without a passenger. I just hoped she didn't do anything stupid before I got back.

Chapter 13

As I rode past the juniper tree I'd been sitting under less than an hour ago, I shuddered thinking of how things would've turned out for Ida if I hadn't decided to ride toward Mosquito Lake and then walk to the top of the hill. It was such an unlikely coincidence.

For the next hour, I checked my phone each time Raven and I crested a hill, but there was no change. We were completely cutoff from the rest of the world. Finally, we reached Three Canyons and were about a half-hour from my vehicle. I checked my phone again. One bar. I let out a whoop, startling my horse, and quickly dialed.

"Sheriff's Office."

"Ira, it's Sarah!" I exclaimed, "I've got an emergency!"

"Who is this? You're cutting out."

"It's Sarah Murdock. Can you hear me now?" *Good grief, I sound like the guy on the commercial.*

"Oh hi, Sarah. What's up?"

"I need you to locate a helicopter and send it to Fee Reservoir to pick me up. I've found that missing protestor."

"What do you need a chopper for? The road goes right up to the water's edge."

"Because she isn't at the reservoir. That's where I'm

headed, but I need a helicopter to meet me there." I could feel my frustration building.

"Well, if she isn't there, why are you going there?"

"Ira!" I shouted. "Shut up and listen. Do you know of a helicopter that can come get me?" Silence on the other end made me think I'd lost the connection.

"Yes." Ira's voice was barely audible. "There's one at the Bieber Helitack Base."

"Great. Call them and get it in the air right now! Tell them to pick me up at Fee Reservoir and be prepared to fly about ten miles into Nevada and then to Alturas. You got that?"

"Yes." A little louder.

"Good." I was about to hang up but stopped. "Thanks, Ira. Sorry I yelled at you." Without waiting for a reply, I disconnected and dialed Remy. It rang twice and then went dead. "Dammit!" I had no idea how long it would take the helicopter to reach Fee Reservoir, but I guessed it wouldn't take much longer than it would take me to get there.

I traded my phone for the water bottle I'd stashed in my fanny pack. As I guzzled the nearly body temperature liquid, Raven turned his head and looked at me over his withers as if pointing out my rudeness of not sharing.

"Sorry," I said, stuffing the empty bottle into one of the saddlebags. "Let's find that spring for you." The gelding nodded his giant head, and we headed west.

Two ridges later, I spotted the watering hole and was relieved to find it vacant. As Raven drank his fill, I tried Remy again. He answered on the second ring, and I quickly explained the situation and asked if he'd be willing to help me.

"Sure thing, partner!" he exclaimed. "I'll be there as quick as I can." Even though he was only about seven miles away, the road consisted mostly of loose gravel, limiting top speed to twenty-five miles per hour or less, so it would take him at least twenty minutes for him to get there.

"I'm about ten minutes away, and I don't know how long it will take the helicopter to get there, so I may already be gone. I'll leave the keys to my truck in the fridge in the horse trailer."

"Got it."

"Thanks, Remy." I snapped my phone shut and we took off again.

Whether the gelding understood the urgency of the situation or just knew he was close to his grain bucket, we made it to the trailer in less than eight minutes. A huge wave of relief swept over me as we crested the last ridge, and I spotted it below us. As quickly as I could, I pulled off his saddle, traded his bridle for a halter and lead rope, and tied him to the shady side of the trailer—not that there was much shade to speak of—making certain the knot was complex enough that he couldn't untie it and free himself before Remy got there. Then I filled a bucket with oats and held it while the gelding ate his snack. I grabbed two more bottles of water out of the backseat of the Dooley, dug my keys out of the fanny pack and was tossing them into the small refrigerator in the sleeper compartment when I heard the rhythmic thwup-thwup-thwup of a helicopter. I headed away from the rig, trying to keep the trailer between Raven and the approaching aircraft in hopes of keeping him as calm as possible.

I'd put almost a hundred yards between us by the time the helicopter was overhead, and I began waving my arms. It hovered for just a few seconds before beginning its descent. I crouched down and waited until it had settled on its skids and the pilot waved me over.

As soon as I climbed in, the copilot handed me a headset, which made communicating over the whirl of the engine and the chop of the blades possible. I strapped myself into the jump seat behind the pilot and pulled on the headset.

"Ready?" a voice asked over the radio.

"Ready," I replied.

The entire helicopter began to shudder as the blades' speed increased, and we lifted off.

"Where are we headed?" a different voice asked.

"Due east, toward Mosquito Lake."

"Roger."

As we swung to the right, I spotted Remy's early model Toyota Land Cruiser bouncing over the dirt road about a quarter of a mile from my rig. Knowing my horse was in good hands, I relaxed a little and hoped that Raven was too tired to give Remy a hard time. Within minutes, the two of them faded from sight, and I turned my attention to the mission at hand.

"We're looking for a huge valley on the east side of this range," I said, twisting in my seat so I could look out of the cockpit windshield. "There's a group of buildings at the base of the last ridge, and that's where we'll find the person we're after."

"Got it."

Less than twenty minutes later, we were circling the location I'd left more than two hours ago. On the second pass, the copilot pointed toward a body laying on the ground. "I thought this was a rescue, not a recovery."

"She's not dead," I replied. *At least I hope she isn't.* "She's hunting."

"She's what?" the copilot said, turning to look at me.

I shook my head. "Never mind. Where are you going to land?"

"Well, looks like the best place is there, to the west of the largest building. What do you think?"

I opened my mouth to answer but closed it quickly when the pilot said, "Roger."

The helicopter banked left and hovered briefly before sinking toward the ground. The body we'd spotted earlier sprang into a sitting position and looked in our direction, using a hand to shade its eyes. Suddenly, it jumped to its feet and started running toward us.

"Uh fellas ... " I said, pointing at the approaching figure.

"Stop right there!" a voice boomed from a speaker mounted somewhere on the outside of the aircraft. "Do not approach until we wave you over." The person, a.k.a. Ida Dudley, skidded to a stop and gave us two thumbs up. *Give me a break!*

"After we set down, you can go get her," the copilot said.

"Copy that."

As soon as the skids came in contact with the ground, I unlatched my belt, left the headset on the seat, and bailed out of the helicopter. I'd only taken a few steps before Ida rushed over, practically knocking me to the ground.

"You *did* come back to get me!" She squealed, throwing her arms around me.

"Of course I did," I replied as I broke free of her embrace and stepped back. "Come on, let's go." I led her back to the waiting aircraft and helped her inside. Seating her on the bench across the back, I made sure her belt was fastened before securing myself back in the jump seat and pulling on the headset. "We're good to go."

"Roger."

Again, the helicopter shuddered as the rotor sped up, and Ida's eyes expanded under her bushy eyebrows, reminding me of the crazed look of her driver's license photo. We rose into the air, and the moment the nose of the helicopter dipped and we headed south, she began speaking and gesturing with her arms, which included pointing out of the cockpit windshield. Turning part way around, I spotted an old homestead consisting of a house and two outbuildings. As we flew over the location, Ida continued to point at it repeatedly and talk very rapidly. Assuming that was the spot where she'd been left, I placed my hands on each side of the headset and shook my head, hoping she would understand that I couldn't hear her. It must have worked because she stopped, leaned back against the seat and closed her eyes.

"So, we're heading for Alturas, right?" the copilot asked.

"Yes," I replied. "And I think it would be a good idea to go straight to the hospital to get her checked out. Do you know where that is?"

"Hold on."

Craning my neck to the right, I watched as he pulled out his smart phone and began searching. A few minutes later, he said, "West side of Main Street on the southern edge of town. Looks like there's a large field where we should be able to set down."

"Roger," the pilot responded.

"Great," I said, relaxing enough to enjoy the scenery as we flew across the expanse of Surprise Valley and up over the jagged peaks of the Warner Mountains. As an FBI agent working out of Quantico, I had flown in a smaller helicopter a couple of times, but this was the first time I'd flown in one this size and with the doors wide open. It almost felt like a ride in a theme park—the air moving past me and the dips and turns of the massive aircraft. I'd just closed my eyes in order to relish the sensation when the helicopter made a sharp, descending right-hand turn and then leveled out. Looking down, I was surprised to see we'd reached the hospital and were preparing to set down in the field the copilot had mentioned earlier.

"Thanks again for the ride, fellas," I said as the helicopter slowly sank toward the ground.

"Our pleasure," the pilot replied. "We were just sitting around, staring at each other."

Chuckling to myself, I again slipped off the headset, released my belt, and stepped over to release Ida's. As soon as the aircraft settled, I hopped out and helped her climb down, assuming her makeshift shoes were unreliable for her to do so on her own. After moving a safe distance away, I turned and waved before leading the rescued protestor into the emergency room.

Chapter 14

"May I help you?" a young woman asked as we approached her desk.

I removed my sunglasses and placed them above the brim of my hat. "I'm Deputy Murdock, and I'd like to have this person checked out, please."

"I was kidnapped!" Ida blurted.

I smiled at the startled registration clerk before turning to my recently rescued victim. "Let's not broadcast that, okay Ida? At least not yet."

She stared at me for a moment or two and then her face changed, like someone who finally understands the punchline of a joke. "Got it," she whispered and winked at me.

Good grief! "She's had a rough week," I said to the clerk.

"A rough week? I was left in the middle of nowhere with no food or water! And I had to make myself a pair of shoes." She held up one of her feet for the clerk to see.

"Ida!"

The woman slowly lowered her leg. "Sorry."

"Uh, I'll need some information before I can send you back," the clerk said, beginning to tap on her keyboard.

"Certainly." I pulled out one of the chairs and motioned for Ida to sit down before making myself comfortable in the other one.

A few minutes and at least twenty questions later, the clerk printed the necessary forms and identifying labels, which she stuck on each page as well as a wristband she deftly attached to Ida's left arm. "Take a seat over there," she said, pointing toward a group of brightly colored chairs, "and someone will be with you shortly."

We moved to the designated area as the clerk disappeared into the restricted section and barely had time to get comfortable before Ida's name was called. The nurse on duty led us down the short hallway and into a small room, where she directed me to a chair in the corner and Ida to the examination bed.

"My name is Jen," she said, placing the file she'd been holding on the small counter, "and I'll be your nurse. Why are we seeing you today?"

"Well, I was kid—"

I quickly interrupted. "Ida! Why don't you let me tell the nurse why you are here." Ignoring her scowl, I continued. "Ida here has spent the past week on her own in the Nevada desert with very little food and water of questionable quality. I located her today and brought her to the hospital for a health check."

"I see," Nurse Jen said. "Let's start with some basics, then." She took Ida's temperature and blood pressure, looked in her ears and down her throat, then made some notations. Next she checked her pupils, pulled down her lower eyelids, and pinched the skin on the back of her hand. "Do you have a headache?" she asked.

"Yes," Ida said, "now that you mention it, I do."

"How about your vision? Does it seem blurry?"

"Not really—well, maybe a little."

"Are you feeling thirsty?"

"Very."

The nurse jotted down some more notes. "I think we are going to need a urine sample. I'll grab a collection cup and be right back." We sat in the quiet until a loud growl came from somewhere deep inside Ida.

"You hungry?" I asked. She grabbed her stomach and nodded her head. "Okay. Just hang on until the doctor examines you, and then we'll get you something to eat."

Before she could answer, there was a brief knock, the door swung open and a woman about my age burst in. Her curly red hair was swept into a messy bun on the top of her head and the chunky earrings dangling from her ears reminded me of a character who drove a magic school bus in some kid's book I'd read as a child.

"Hello, I'm Dr. Frances Hood, but you can call me Dr. Franny." She scanned Ida's file for a moment. "So, it looks like you've been on an adventure. Are you injured anywhere?" Ida shook her head. "And what's going on here?" The doctor asked, pointing to her feet.

"Oh, those are the shoes I had to make for myself."

"I see. May I take a look?"

"Sure," Ida said, holding out both feet.

The doctor swung Ida's legs around and placed them on the bed. Then she carefully removed her socks, one after the other. The toes and edges of each foot were a strange lavender color. Folds of some kind of material and small wooden planks were bound to her feet with straps of electrical tape that were wrapped so tightly the flesh on the top of each foot bulged between them.

"What is wrong with her feet?" I asked, leaning forward to get a closer look.

"Well, I think it has something to do with how tightly this tape has been wrapped around them." The doctor began looking through the drawers of a roll-around cabinet. "How long have you had your feet bound like this?" she asked after locating a strange pair of scissors with angled blades.

"Umm, I think I made my shoes on Wednesday or Thursday, but I'm not sure," Ida said. "It was two or three days after I was kidnapped."

"You were what?"

Before I could explain, the door opened and the nurse stepped into the room. "I have the collection... " She stopped as soon as she looked in Ida's direction. "Yikes! What's wrong with her feet?"

"Looks like peripheral cyanosis due to poor perfusion," Dr. Franny said as she began cutting the tape on Ida's feet. "We are going to need warm fluids and a heated blanket."

"Right away, Doctor," the nurse said, placing the collection cup on the counter and leaving again.

Dr. Franny cut through each strap of tape on Ida's feet and slowly peeled them back, revealing bright red welts across the top of each foot. "Didn't you feel a tingling in your feet when you did this?"

"Only at first, but then it went away." Ida studied her feet. "Oh my, that doesn't look good."

"No, it does not," the doctor agreed. "I usually see

this with diabetic patients. Sometimes this condition can cause blood clots that can travel to the heart or lungs. We'll get treatment started, but I think we need to admit you for a few days just to be sure there aren't any complications."

"Complications?" Ida's face began to get that crazed look again.

"Just as a precaution," Dr. Franny reassured her.

The nurse returned with a clear plastic bag filled with some kind of fluid and coils of tubing balanced on top of a folded, thin white blanket. She dumped her load on the counter and began rummaging through the drawers where the doctor had found the scissors. Locating what she was looking for, she turned around. "Now, let's get your IV started."

My strong aversion to needles of any kind made me realize that was my cue to leave. "Well Ida, looks like you're in good hands, so I'm going to take off. I'll come back tomorrow to check on you." On my way out, I left my name with instructions to contact the Sheriff's Office if they needed to reach me.

Pushing through the door and into the glare of midday, I replaced my sunglasses and retrieved my cell phone from my fanny pack.

"Hey Remy," I said when he answered. "How about a ride home?"

"You bet, partner. Where are you?"

"I'm at the hospital out on West McDowell Avenue." My stomach rumbled. "But I think I'll walk over to the burger joint on the edge of town and grab some lunch."

"You mean The Burger Pitt?"

"Yeah, that's the place."

"Alrighty then, I'll... Now hang on young fella... for the love of... "

"Remy?"

"Somebody will be there in a jiffy."

"Great, thanks." I hung up and started toward Main Street. *Somebody? Must have misunderstood him.*

Within a few minutes, I'd reached the Pitt and stepped inside. The cool interior was a pleasant break from the heat, and I quickly realized it was the perfect place to wait the hour it would take *somebody* to come get me.

I stood in line, contemplating my numerous choices but settled for my usual selection when it became my turn to order. "Double bacon-cheeseburger, fries and a chocolate malt, please."

The female teenager behind the counter punched a few buttons on the electronic cash register. "That will be $9.32."

I reached for my Filson leather snap wallet in the hip pocket of my jeans, but since I had on knee-length compression shorts instead, it wasn't there. I started to unzip my fanny pack when I remembered that my wallet was safely tucked away in the center console of my Ford Dooley, which by now should be parked in my driveway. *Dammit!* "Um, I don't seem to have my wallet on me at the moment."

The girl crossed her arms over her chest and stared at me.

"But I can pay in about an hour when my ride gets here." I flashed her a big smile and tried to look as honest and sincere as I could.

She shook her head. "I'm not supposed to give anyone credit."

"Come on, Bambi... "

"My name's Barbie," she interrupted.

Oh, great way to make points. "Sorry, Barbie—but you know me. I've been in here several times."

"I don't think so," she began, slowly shaking her head again.

That's when I realized most of my face was hidden behind my sunglasses and the floppy brim of my bush hat. I quickly removed them and smiled. "See? I'm usually wearing my uniform."

"Uniform?"

"Deputy Murdock," I said, patting my chest like I was trying to communicate with someone who didn't speak English.

Seconds ticked by and then, "Oh yeah, Deputy," she said, nodding vigorously. "No cash, huh?"

"Yeah," I sighed. "No cash. At least not at the moment."

"That's okay. I'll go ahead and put in your order, and you can pay me when your cash gets here."

"Great, thanks." I moved away from the counter and sat at a small booth near the front window.

By the time I'd eaten my burger as well as most of the fries and was down to the last few slurps of my milkshake, *nobody* had shown up to get me. I finished off my meal and threw away the trash. Unable to do anything but wait, I returned to my table, replaced my hat and sunglasses, and propped myself against the window.

I don't know how long I was asleep, but when I woke up, Pete was sitting across from me. "Where did you come from?" I asked, straightening up and stretching my arms above my head.

"I'm your ride home."

"Oh, so you're *somebody*."

"Yeah," he chuckled. "Remy called me to help retrieve his Land Cruiser after he got your truck and trailer back to your place." He paused as Barbie placed a tray of food in front of him. "He wasn't too happy that I showed up on my Harley, but there was no way I was taking my GTO on that road." He took a bite of his burger, and I waited for him to go on. "Anyway, we ended up taking his quad, but on the way back, I was having some fun, going over a couple of jumps and that ticked him off some more." Another bite and more waiting. "We'd just gotten back to his place when you called."

"That phone call was a bit strange."

Pete nodded as he chewed his most recent bite. "I offered to come get you, and that made him even madder."

I recalled a time when Remy thought my sister, who was visiting at the time, was trying to take his place on an investigation we'd started together. "Yeah, he doesn't like it when he feels he's getting left out."

"Well, I'm sure it will be some time before he asks me for help again." He finished his burger and washed it down with most of his soda. "Ready?"

"Sure." I started for the door and then remembered I had some unfinished business. "Oh wait, I almost forgot. Can I borrow ten dollars?"

"Nope," he said, shaking his head.

"But I... "

"All taken care of."

"But how... "

"When I placed my order, I happened to mention I was here to pick up Sleeping Beauty." He winked at me. "And the gal over there let me know you still owed for your lunch, so I paid her."

"Oh thanks, Pete."

"No problemo. Besides, I know you're good for it."

"Humph, we'll see," I said, tossing my head like I'd seen my sister, Alexis, do a thousand times. However, without her perfectly styled blond hair or her designer clothes, I doubt it had the same effect. Not waiting to find out, I pushed through the door and started across the parking lot.

"Wow, your bike really looks great," I said as we approached the Harley motorcycle that was once again black with gold trim. "You'd never know it had been spray-painted red." *Or stolen or had saddlebags installed on it.* I was just glad he'd gotten it back in one piece.

"I've been waiting to take my baby out for a road trip, which is why I really wanted to come get you. Seemed like the perfect opportunity." He unhooked a skull cap helmet from the side of the bike and handed it to me. "Here you go. Gotta keep my passenger safe."

"Why thank you, kind sir." I pulled off my hat and stuffed it into my fanny pack before strapping on the helmet. Pete pulled on his own full face helmet and straddled the bike. I hopped on behind him and soon we were speeding along, climbing the mountain toward Cedar Pass.

It was just after two-thirty when we pulled into Remy's driveway to pick up Bubbles, but before I could fetch him, the front door opened just enough to let my small dog out and then slammed shut.

Unbelievable! "Thank you, Remy!" I called, uncertain whether or not he'd heard me. *Hope he cools off soon.* Bubbles trotted around us a couple of times until I could coax him to jump into my arms. Minutes later we coasted down my own driveway and parked in the shade of the huge cottonwood tree that grew next to my house.

"So what do you have planned for the rest of today?" Pete asked, taking the loaner helmet from me and hanging it on the handlebars next to his.

"Soak in the hot tub until I'm a raisin," I said, after retrieving my wallet and keys from the Dooley and unlocking my front door.

"Isn't it too hot for that?"

I grinned at him. "Not if you fill it with cooler water."

"Sounds good. Count me in."

"How about you?" I asked the miniature mutt at my feet. "You in?"

A change of clothes and a couple of beers later, the three of us floated weightlessly in the crystal-clear water. The perfect way to end one hell of a day!

Chapter 15

I poured myself another cup of coffee and sat at the desk in my office. Munching on a protein bar, I opened my notebook to a blank page and jotted down the information Ida had provided about her kidnapping; getting gas at Rabbit Traxx, a bag being pulled over her head, screaming for help and banging on the side of the trailer, given some kind of an injection and waking up in the abandoned farm house without shoes or socks. Still not much to go on. *Hopefully, she'll think of something that'll be more useful.*

"Come on, Bubbles," I called, setting my half-finished coffee in the sink. "Time to go."

As I pulled into Remy's driveway, I didn't see him anywhere. However, as soon as I stepped out of my patrol unit, the front door opened just enough to admit the small dog that had jumped out after me. As soon as Bubbles was inside, it slammed shut, a good indication that Remy was still upset with the whole Pete situation.

I waved good-bye just in case before climbing back into the Explorer and headed for Alturas. An uneventful trip, I parked near the main entrance to the hospital and grabbed my cell phone. Keeping my promise, I dialed the number for the *Alturas Gazette* and asked for Lulu DeLoure.

I identified myself as soon as she came on the line and asked, "Remember that picture of the missing person you helped get in the paper?"

"Yes."

"Well, I found her."

"You did?"

"Yes, she's at the hospital. I'm here now if you want to come talk to her."

"Be right there!" And she hung up.

Still feeling Lulu's involvement might be a bad idea, I went inside to find Ida. Two inquiries and three hallways later, I found her enjoying the last of her morning meal. "Hello, Ida. Doing better today?"

"Oh yes, much! This is the best breakfast I've had in months."

Fairly certain it was go-to-the-freezer-and-get-the-box food, I wondered what kind of swill she'd been consuming. "And how are your feet?"

"I'm not sure. I haven't looked at them yet." She pushed the covers down to her knees and pulled out one foot. "It almost looks normal."

I had to agree. Most of the discoloration was gone, leaving only a few reddish splotches on her pinky toe.

"Sure hurt, though. Felt like they were on fire for a while."

"I imagine it did." I tugged my notebook out of my hip pocket and opened it to the notes I'd made earlier that morning. "Feel up to answering a couple of questions for me?"

"Sure." She tucked her foot back under the covers, finished off her orange juice, and pushed her tray aside. "Go ahead."

But before I could begin, some kind of disturbance started happening, so I excused myself and stepped into the hallway. I spotted the tuft of neon pink hair right away, adorning the reporter who was trying to push past the two nurses standing in her way.

"But I'm supposed to be interviewing the victim. You have to let me pass."

Before things got too out of hand, I hurried toward them "Excuse me ladies, it's all right to let Miss Deloure pass."

"Thank you... " she said, "and please call me Lulu." She readjusted the strap of her bag higher onto her shoulder, tucking it under the ruffled collar of her pale yellow blouse and tugged at her green plaid pencil skirt. I led the way to Ida's room and Lulu followed, her brown pumps with their three inch heels clacking on the linoleum.

"Ida," I said as I re-entered her room, "this is Lulu DeLoure. She's a reporter with the *Alturas Gazette*."

"A reporter?"

"Yes, she's here to do a story about your rescue. But first," I began, looking at Lulu, "I need to ask Ida a few more questions."

"Gotcha," Lulu said as she sat down in the nearest chair. She dropped her bag on the floor next to her and began rummaging through it.

"Now," I said, focusing on Ida again, "I understand that you were grabbed while getting gas and that someone threw a bag over your head and tossed you in a trailer."

"Oh my!" Lulu interjected.

"Yes, that's right."

"Why didn't you try to get out?" I asked.

"I couldn't move my arms. He must have tied them somehow."

"I see." I retrieved my pen, jotted down this new information, and glanced at Lulu, who was hastily scribbling in her own notebook.

"Did the person who grabbed you say anything?" I asked.

"Yes," Ida replied. "He called me the b-word and said some rather nasty things about me and what should happen to me."

"Awful!" Lulu again.

"Had you heard his voice before? Did you recognize it?"

Ida pondered for a moment. "You know, it kinda sounded like that actor that's been in all those cowboy movies."

Only one name came to mind. "John Wayne?"

"No, no," Ida said. "He has a big mustache and speaks slowly with a deep voice."

"Sam Elliot," Lulu offered, still scribbling away.

"Yes, that's him." Ida agreed. "That's exactly who he sounded like."

I tried to recall the voices of the cowboys I'd spoken to at the roundup and then later at the Sheriff's Office, but nothing stood out. "Okay, is there anything else you can tell me that I might not have covered?"

"Not that I can think of."

Lulu got to the end of the sentence she'd been writing and looked up. "Officer... "

"Deputy," I interrupted. "Deputy Murdock."

"Got it." She scratched out something in her notes. "Can you tell me how... " She referred to her notes again. "How Ida got rescued?"

"Sure. I was riding my horse east of Fee Reservoir, and I found her at a building complex in a remote location. After giving her some food, I rode back the way I'd come until I could use my phone to request a helicopter, which then picked me up at the reservoir, flew back to where I'd left her, picked her up and flew us directly to this hospital."

Lulu, her pen flying across the pages of her notebook, continuously nodded her head and muttered "Uh-huh," until she got to the end of my tale. "Wow, what were the odds of you finding her?" she asked.

"Too many for me to think about," I said, tucking my notebook back in my pocket. "Ida, I have some things I have to do, so I will see you later." I moved toward the door. "And, Miss DeLoure... " *Sometimes, I just can't help myself!* "... I look forward to reading your story." Then I left.

I arrived at the office about fifteen minutes later, after a brief stop at the market to grab a salad in a box for lunch. As I passed by the dispatcher's desk, I noticed Cindy was on the phone, so I proceeded down the hall to the small conference room where I planned to write my report. I'd just booted up the computer and opened my notebook when she appeared in the doorway.

"You weren't even going to stop and fill me in?" she asked.

"Fill you in on what?"

"You know what," she said, crossing her arms over her chest. "That missing protestor you found."

"Oh, not much to tell," I began, trying desperately to keep a straight face.

She looked up and down the hall, entered the room and dropped into the chair next to me. "Now spill it!"

"Well, I found her, and I brought her back to... "

"Sarah!" Cindy interrupted. "You know there's more to it than that. Fee Reservoir, a helicopter, the Nevada desert, some kind of rescue," she said, ticking each item off on her fingers.

I laughed. *So Ira was paying attention.*

"Start at the beginning. I want all the details, don't—" An incoming call interrupted her. "Dammit! I'll be right back." While she was gone, I got started on my report and, each time she left to answer the phone, I worked on it. Telling the story actually helped me recall the details and, by the end of the fifth phone call, it was done. "Got any suspects?" Cindy asked when I finished telling her my story.

"You know, that's the most frustrating part. Based on an eyewitness account, a dark-colored truck and white or silver trailer was spotted around the time of Ida's disappearance, which is corroborated by her own statement. However, the surveillance tape at the gas station doesn't show enough to determine make or model of the truck or the trailer," I said as I saved my report to the flash drive I carried on my key ring and sent it to the main copier to be printed. "She claims she didn't see who grabbed her, but he spoke to her."

"Well, that'll help won't it?"

"Based on what she told me, I should be issuing a warrant for the arrest of Sam Elliot."

Cindy tilted her head to one side and frowned. "What?"

"Ida says the guy sounded like Sam Elliot."

"Oh man," Cindy chuckled. "There's no other evidence? What about where she was dumped?"

I began to shake my head and then stopped. "To be honest, I'm not sure. Where I found her was not where she got dumped, and I didn't have time then to go look around." I popped the top on my salad, tore open the dressing and squeezed it onto my salad. "You know," I said as I stirred it around, "it might not hurt to go check it out. Make sure there isn't any evidence indicating who took her."

"Sounds like a good idea to me," Cindy agreed. "Just wish I could go with you."

"Yeah, that would be an adventure, for sure." *And maybe I know someone else who'd like to tag along.*

Chapter 16

I turned onto County Road 224 and flew past Remy's driveway, heading toward my place. I needed to check the map hanging on the wall of my office and plot the best course to the old farm house where Ida had been dumped.

After locating Mosquito Lake again, this time I followed the road back toward Fort Bidwell. Starting there, I moved back toward the east and jotted down some notes. Taking the familiar Fee Reservoir Road, I would veer left onto Barrel Springs Road and follow it past Big Mud Lake and into Nevada. Then I'd travel down what looked like a switchback into the valley where the road passes through Mosquito Lake and then connects with Fort Bidwell Road, before continuing south past Cow-Camp Road. Not sure of the exact location where I'd found Ida, I fired up my computer, accessed Google Maps and selected the satellite option. Zooming in, I spotted the building complex I'd come across the day before. Slowly sliding the map, another group of buildings came into view. I zoomed in again and was confident I'd found the place Ida had pointed out as we'd flown over in the helicopter. Reading through my notes as I looked at the satellite image, I felt fairly certain I'd be able to get to my destination without getting lost, but to be on the safe side, I grabbed my GPS.

I still had a partial case of water in the back of my patrol unit, so I grabbed what was left of my apples and a couple of protein bars, even though I would've preferred a bag of Doritos and a candy bar, and headed back to Remy's.

The greeting I received when I pulled into his driveway was icy, to say the least, in spite of the warm weather. He stood at the bottom of his front steps, his arms crossed over his white T-shirt, having abandoned the customary long sleeve plaid shirt, and he had a frown on his face. "You already done with your day?" he asked when I climbed out of the Explorer.

"Not exactly," I replied, stepping closer. "I just came to pick up Bubbles. I have to drive out to the spot where that protestor got dumped and check for any evidence. Thought the dog might like to ride along."

"Evidence, huh?" Remy let his arms drop to his sides. "Is it a fur piece?"

"At least an hour's drive from here I think, depending on the road. That's why I thought I might as well take the dog. I think he misses riding around with me."

"Yeah, I 'spect he does." He pulled out a blue and white handkerchief, mopped at the beads of sweat on his forehead and shoved it back into his hip pocket. "You...uh... sure there won't be any danger? No need for backup?"

That's the partner I know! "Well, it has been over a week since she was dumped there, so probably not dangerous."

Remy's facial expression melted like an ice cream cone on a hot day.

"But," I quickly added, "I might need some help looking for evidence. Don't want to miss anything."

The grin that emerge on the old gentleman's face made his beard and mustache expand. "Give me just a couple of minutes to grab a few things, and I'll be right with you." He hurried up the steps and entered the front door, dodging around Bubbles and Millie as they rushed out to play.

While I waited, I loaded Bubbles into the backseat, took off my gun belt and stashed it under my seat, figuring it would be rather uncomfortable on the long, bumpy ride. Moments later, Remy reappeared, carrying a small soft-sided ice chest and a blue plaid shirt.

"Just grabbed us a light snack for the road," he said, opening the back door on the passenger side and setting the ice chest on the floor. He slipped on the shirt but left it unbuttoned. "Come on, Millie."

"Millie?" I watched as the small goat gracefully leapt into the backseat.

"Why sure! She loves to ride in vehicles." He closed the door and climbed into the passenger seat. "Besides, she'll be good company for Bubbles."

Shaking my head and questioning my sanity, I slid in behind the wheel and started my patrol unit. Within minutes, we were traveling on the gravel roadway, enjoying the coolness of the air-conditioned interior and headed for Nevada.

"I'm pretty sure this is the valley we're looking for," I said as we briefly stopped at the top of the switchback that would take us down the face of the small mountain and to the edge of Mosquito Lake.

"This here road looks like it could be a might treacherous," Remy said, leaning forward to get a better look. "One wrong move and..." He whistled a sound resembling a bomb dropping.

"Well, fortunately for us, it's a dry hot day, and I'm driving." On the satellite picture, the road looked similar to the one I travel to Fandango Pass, but seen in person, it was not as wide nor as heavily graveled and best avoided during inclement weather.

As we crossed the lake, the road narrowed and passed along the top of a small levee. "Hells bells," Remy declared. "In a wet year, I'd wager this here part of the road disappears."

"Definitely a fair-weather thoroughfare," I agreed.

A quarter of a mile further, I spotted a familiar complex at the base of a hill to the right of us. "That's where I found Ida," I said, pointing it out to Remy. "They call the road going into there Cow-Camp Road, so I can only assume the place is referred to as Cow Camp."

He nodded. "Makes sense."

"And our destination should be just on the other side of that knoll dead ahead of us."

"Alrighty then, let's get to it." His enthusiasm was a clear indicator that he was over being angry and ready for the next adventure.

I pulled over before we reached the abandoned farm house. "You and the animals sit tight for a few minutes. I want to take a look for tire tracks and footprints first. When I signal you, go ahead and drive to the entrance but stay on the road."

"Will do."

I climbed out and moved to the back of my rig to retrieve my digital camera. Scanning both sides of the road, I approached the entrance to the property. There was no evidence to suggest any kind of vehicle had pulled to one side of the road or the other. The opening in the fence had been secured with a portagee gate but the top loop was undone, allowing it to lean against the dried grass stalks that measured three to four feet and covered almost every inch of the property.

Between the road and the gate, there were a few scuffs and indentations in the the dirt, but nothing distinctive enough to be labeled a footprint. I pushed through the opening and continued looking for any indication that that someone had done the same but found nothing. The vegetation was just too thick.

Before going any further, I signaled Remy. While I waited for him to bring the rig down, I stepped over to check out the closest building. It actually looked like three separate structures that had been shoved together and connected. The longest section had a dirt floor, shed roof, and had been divided into stalls. The smallest section also had a dirt floor and shed roof and reminded me of a covered pigsty on my uncle's farm. The last section was more substantially built with a gable roof and well-worn plank floor. Letting my eyes adjust to the dark interior, I could make out the prints of human bare feet in the dust that had accumulated on the floor. Judging from the erratic pattern, I assumed they had been made by the missing protestor before taping the material and wooden planks to her feet for shoes. As I stepped back out into the bright sunshine, I was joined by a small dog, a white goat, and an energetic old man.

"Find anything?" he asked.

"Just some footprints that I'm sure Ida made herself," I replied, nodding toward the building I'd just explored.

"Oh." Major disappointment. "Maybe there's clues in one of the other buildings. Come on." Remy led the way, pushing through the tall, dead grass like a trailblazer cutting a path through the jungle. Just as he reached the open door of what I assumed was the main house, I reached out and took hold of his shoulder. "Hold up a sec," I said. "Let me go first in case there are any recognizable footprints."

Reluctantly, he stepped out of my way, and I went inside. The walls and floor had, at one time, been whitewashed and therefore, did not readily reveal any dust let alone footprints. The two smaller rooms toward the back contained nothing more than a few dead leaves scattered around. A ladder built into the wall between them led to a loft directly above. Given the condition of the wood, I declined the opportunity to investigate that area further. The main room also had accumulations of dead leaves here and there, and part of a wood burning cookstove lay on its side beneath where the missing stove pipe would have passed through the roof. An old, chipped enameled sink was mounted to the wall with a makeshift bracket. Next to it, a rusty water hand pump was bolted to the narrow counter. I stepped over and gave the handle a couple of pumps, but nothing happened.

"Doubt you'll get a single drop outta that," Remy said,

shaking his head. "Most likely the well's dry, and if it's not, air's probably gotten into the system, breaking the suction." He stepped closer and gave it a couple of pumps himself. "Yeah, my folks had one of these here contraptions when I was a kid. My dad was always having to mess with it." He looked around. "That there woman was lucky to make it to a place that had water."

I had to agree. Luck seemed to be something Ida Dudley had plenty of—except for being kidnapped, that is. "I doubt we'll find anything else, but let's finish looking around and head back," I suggested.

"Sounds good to me."

The only other items in the room were a broken shovel handle, a few loops of baling wire, some pieces of what looked like cedar shake roofing, and a short piece of chain piled in the center of the floor. A tour of the outside revealed a lean-to attached to the north side of the house surrounded by a fenced in area. Most likely used to house animals, it was now completely hidden by vegetation. Another small shed, with the lower portion of its back wall missing, had been built a short distance from the house. An outhouse, engulfed by a scraggly apple tree, was precariously tipped to the right.

"My guess is the pit underneath is giving way," Remy said, nodding at the small decaying building. He chuckled. "Dug a few of them in my lifetime. All this investigating got me hungry. You 'bout ready for a snack?"

"Might as well," I replied. "This was a bust as far as gathering any useful evidence." We began the trek back to the Explorer. "I've got some apples and protein bars to share."

"That's mighty generous of you, but I have something a bit more substantial."

As I stowed my camera, he ushered the animals into the backseat and grabbed the ice chest. Placing it on the floorboard between his feet, he began pulling out plastic containers and setting them on the console. Then he handed me a fork and a napkin. "We've got some cold, fried chicken and coleslaw, and for dessert..." He reached into the ice chest again and removed two more small containers. "...apple Brown Betty!"

My mouth watered, and my stomach growled so loudly that I'm sure Remy heard it. It was as if I hadn't even had a salad for lunch.

"Grab one of your apples for Millie, and I'll tear off a few hunks of chicken for Bubba, and soon as a couple of these here containers are empty, we'll fill 'em with one of your bottles of water."

"Do you want a water?"

"Got something better than that." He reached into the seemingly bottomless ice chest and pulled out two pint-size jars filled with a brown liquid and a few floating ice cubes.

"What's that?" I asked.

"Sweet tea, made using Peg's world-famous recipe."

I did as I was told and fetched an apple and a bottle of water, and we all enjoyed the feast he'd brought.

Chapter 17

"**D**id you say someone called to report too many horses?" I released the button on the mic and dropped it into my lap. Certain I'd misunderstood Cindy, I pulled over in front of the motel on the western edge of Cedarville. I'd been patrolling toward Cedar Pass when I got the call.

"That's right," she said. "RP says there's an extra horse in the pasture that's not his."

I retrieved the mic and pressed the transmission button. "Okay, give me the location again."

"Take the first road to the right just north of Upper Lake City Road on County Road 1. RP will be waiting near a partially collapsed barn."

"Got it, 113 responding."

"Copy. Time is 8:26."

I turned around and drove back to the four-way stop in the center of Cedarville. Taking a left, I headed north and reached the turnoff a few minutes later. As I approached the dilapidated building, I noticed two trucks, each towing a livestock trailer, parked nearby. Neither was dark-colored with a light-colored trailer. Four men of various ages stood near a small corral where several horses were being held. One of the men stepped forward as I pulled up.

"Fred Fredrickson," he said, extending his right hand.

Fredrickson? The name sounded familiar, but nothing clicked as to why. "Deputy Murdock," I replied, shaking his hand. "I understand you have an extra horse."

"That's right." He started toward the corral. "We have eight horses that we rotate on our smaller fields, but as you can see..." He paused as he pointed at the group of animals. "...we've gathered nine."

I reached into my hip pocket and retrieved my notebook. "Do you have any idea where the horse may have come from? Does it look familiar?"

Fred shook his head. "We mostly run quarter horses, but this one," he said, indicating the extra animal, "definitely isn't a quarter horse." At least a hand shorter, the dark brown animal also had a slighter build than the others. "The only thing I can tell you is that it's a wild horse that's been rounded up by the BLM and adopted out."

"How do you know?"

"There's a freeze brand on its neck, underneath the mane."

Apparently my education of wild horses at the roundup was interrupted before freeze brands were covered. Fortunately, I was fairly sure I had someone to ask. "Any idea when it may have been put here?"

"Nope, sorry. I mean, we drive by here a lot but usually just glance over to make sure the horses are still there. You see, we move them every couple of months."

"And so I assume it's time, and that's why the trailers are here."

"You got it. And so the last time I knew exactly how many horses were in this field was the end of July when we put them here."

"Understood," I said, nodding my head. "Where are you moving them this time?"

"Back to the ranch, south of Lake City."

"Is that on the main road?" I didn't know why, but I had a gut feeling that the horse was somehow connected to my kidnapping investigation. The sudden appearance of an adopted BLM mustang so soon after the roundup couldn't be just a coincidence.

"Actually, it's on County Road 142 and runs along the base of the Warners," Fred said as he adjusted his ball cap and folded his arms across his chest.

Perfect! "Until I can track down who the horse belongs to, if that's even possible, would you mind keeping it?"

Fred removed his ball cap and ran his hand over his closely cropped hair before replacing it. "I suppose we can do that, as long as it isn't for an extended amount of time."

"Give me a week, two at the most. And if I haven't located the owner by then, I'll come get it myself."

"Fair enough." He turned to the other men who were still standing near the corral. "All right boys, let's get 'em loaded. Bud, catch that mustang so the deputy here can take a look at that freeze brand."

"Sure thing, Mr. Fredrickson," the young man replied. He grabbed a halter and lead rope that had been hanging on the side of the corral and slipped inside. Moving quickly, he reached the head of the horse and had the halter in place within seconds and led the animal to where I was waiting.

Sweeping its mane to the other side of its neck, I was surprised to find symbols resembling cuneiform writing rather than an alphanumeric serial number. I copied it into my notebook but had some doubts as to my accuracy. "Hang on a second," I told Bud, "I want to get a picture of it as well."

"Why don't you just use your phone?" he asked as I turned toward my patrol unit. I pulled out the flip phone I could barely text on and held it up. "Oh," he snickered, "never mind."

I'd received previous ribbings from Cindy about my technologically simple phone, but for the most part just ignored her. *Perhaps an upgrade someday might be prudent.* In the meantime, I'd have to rely on the digital camera I carried in my evidence case. When I got back to the corral, the other horses had been loaded, and one of the trucks was starting to pull out. I took a few pictures, thanked Fred again for keeping the extra horse, and returned to the Explorer. But before continuing with my patrol, I made a phone call.

"Hi, Bonnie, this is Sarah Murdock," I said when she answered. "How are things with the BLM?"

"Oh, same as always. Managing and maintaining your public land."

"Awesome," I chuckled. "Hey, I was hoping you could help me out with something. Is there a way to determine who adopted a wild horse by looking at its freeze brand?"

"I think so." She paused. "Does this have anything to do with that missing protestor?"

"I'm not sure. A rancher has discovered an extra horse in his field, and turns out it's a mustang with a freeze brand on its neck. My gut is telling me that somehow it's related to my investigation."

"Ah, good old woman's intuition, huh?"

Anger flooded my brain as I flashed on an old nemesis from my past, but it quickly passed. "Yeah, that's right—woman's intuition. Anyway, think you might be able to help me?"

"I'm stuck in the office today, so if you want to bring it by, I'll see what I can find out."

"That would be great. See you in a few." I snapped shut my outdated flip phone, followed the second livestock trailer back to the main road, and again headed for Cedarville.

When I entered the BLM office on Cressler Street, Bonnie was leaning against the front counter, talking with the receptionist. "You weren't kidding when you said you'd be here soon. Come on, we'll go back to my office." She led the way down a narrow hallway and into a very cluttered room. "You'll have to excuse the mess. I never seem to have enough space."

The wooden desk, which faced the small window, was almost completely hidden by piles of paper as well as a variety of stacking trays and baskets stuffed with folders, one of which was held down by a large tarantula forever entombed in a dome of acrylic. Her computer monitor was covered with a rainbow of sticky notes, and small bottles filled with what I assumed were samples of some kind occupied any remaining space of the desktop. File boxes, some stacked four high, lined the perimeter of the small office, and maps and charts of indigenous flora and fauna covered the walls. After clearing off the spare chair, she dragged it over to her desk and motioned for me to sit down. "Let's see what you have," she said, extending the slide-out writing surface. I showed her the symbols I'd written down. "Okay, this first figure tells us that the horse is from the United States. See these next two that look like stacked equal signs, one vertical and one horizontal? That's the approximate year it was born." She reached toward her computer and retrieved a laminated card and laid it next to my notebook. Something resembling an eight-point star was printed on it, with a different number written in each point and a set of equal signs resembling the ones I'd written down were in the center, along with the numbers one and zero. "Looking at this key decoder, it looks like your horse was born around 2010. The next two symbols tell where the horse is from." She wrote down the numbers two and four under their corresponding symbols. "The rest of this," she said as she began translating the remaining symbols to numbers, "is the registration number assigned to the person who adopted the horse." She stopped writing and leaned closer to my notebook. "I can't tell if this is a nine or an eight," she said, pointing at the next to last symbol I had written down. "It's hard to tell the exact position of the angle."

"I took a picture of it, if you want to see it?" I offered. "It's on the SD card in my camera."

"Sure. I have a port for it on my computer."

After stepping out to my patrol unit, I was surprised to find Bonnie sitting on the floor and partially under her desk when I returned to her office. "Having the computer stack under my desk isn't always convenient," she said, holding out her hand. Obviously interpreting the expression on my face she continued. "Makes plugging anything into it quite challenging." She inserted the SD card I'd handed her and returned to her chair. A few clicks later, a photo of the freeze brand appeared on her monitor. "Sometimes as the hair grows, the symbols get muddied. Some get so bad you have to shave the spot to see them clearly." She enlarged the picture. "It's still hard to determine for certain what number this one is," she said, tapping on the screen.

"Oh, great. How can we find out which it is?" I asked.

"Well, I think the best thing to do is write it down twice, once with a nine and once with an eight." Bonnie grabbed one of her many colorful pads of sticky notes. "I'll have to contact someone who deals with the adoption program and see if they can access the national database," she replied, jotting down the two versions of the sequence of numbers she'd just decoded. "It might take a few days." She removed my SD card from her computer and handed it to me.

"That's fine. The horse isn't going anywhere, and this may just be another dead end anyway. Give me a call if you have any luck." I stood and put the chair back. "Thanks for your help."

"Sure thing."

I returned to my patrol, hopeful that I might finally get a break in my investigation.

Chapter 18

The day seemed to drag on and constantly checking my phone wasn't helping. Anxious to receive information from Bonnie regarding the wild horse, I'd placed it in the cupholder where it remained silent for most of the day. Finally, within minutes of the end of my shift, it signaled that I'd received a text.

After pulling to the side of the road near the airport, I snatched up the phone and flipped it open. The message was from Pete, asking me to stop by the Spur before heading home. Feeling strangely disappointed, I made a U-turn and returned to Cedarville.

The cool, dark interior was as inviting as ever, and as I approached my usual spot at the bar, I nodded at the small group of local ranchers sitting around a table near the small stage. The only other customer was a guy sitting at the end of the bar closest to the pool table.

"Howdy Deputy," Pete said when he saw me. "That was quick."

"Hey, Pete." I climbed onto the barstool I'd begun to think of as my own. "I was just up the road when I got your text. What's up?"

Pete poured each of us a cup of the thick, black liquid he called coffee and put them on the bar between us. Then he grabbed a handful of sugar packets and the half-and-half out of the refrigerator unit and placed them near my cup. "I'm afraid I have some bad news."

"Oh?" I tore open the packets and dumped them into my coffee.

"So, my parents' 50th anniversary is coming up and my brother and sister have been pressuring me to come home for the celebration." He handed me the long metal spoon he uses to stir mixed drinks.

"Thanks." I added a splash of half-and-half and stirred the concoction. "When is it?"

He stared at me for a moment and then said, "This weekend."

"But the endurance competition is this weekend!"

"I know, I know," Pete said, holding up both hands in surrender, "and I'm really sorry, but my siblings are not taking no for an answer. I'm leaving tomorrow and I won't be back until sometime next week. I'm really sorry."

"But..."

"Believe me," Pete interrupted, "I'd much rather go with you but there's no way to get out of it without having my whole family pissed off at me again."

"Well, yeah I can see—wait...what? Pissed off at you, again?"

Pete chuckled. "Remember I told you I was supposed to become a preacher like my father, but instead I hitch-hiked to California to pursue my love of music?"

I slowly nodded.

"Well, it wasn't like I did it with their blessing. They didn't speak to me for three years after that. And that was because my younger brother got ordained. Then, all of a sudden, it was like I was forgiven or something," he said, shaking his head. "Go figure."

If I was going to the competition alone, not having Pete there wouldn't really matter as I was used to managing by myself. But with Scott tagging along, I was counting on having someone else to help keep him in line. "Well, dammit!" I slid off my stool and headed for the bathroom. As I glanced down the bar, the man at the end turned slightly away from me and pulled his ball cap down, obscuring his face, but urgent business in the small room near the front door prevented me from investigating the somewhat suspicious behavior. By the time I returned to my place at the bar, he was gone. "Do you know who was sitting at the end of the bar?" I asked Pete. "I didn't recognize him."

"No clue," he said. "He's been coming in to have a beer or two every day for about a week. Keeps to himself, mostly. Why?"

Because he somehow looks familiar and was acting suspicious! But instead I answered, "Oh, no reason. Well, guess I should be heading home."

As I began to dismount, Pete reached out and placed his hand over mine. "I really am sorry, and I promise I'll make it up to you."

I smiled at him. "I know you are, and I'm looking forward to it."

Climbing back into my patrol unit, I checked my phone, which I'd left in the cupholder. Nothing. No texts. No missed calls. *The disappointments just keep piling up!* Anxious to purge the day's frustrations with a vigorous workout followed by a soak in the hot tub, I fired up the engine and headed north.

Thirty minutes later, I pulled into Remy's driveway to collect my canine companion and was greeted almost immediately by the trio that hung out there.

"You're home a little later than usual," Remy said when he strolled over. "Were you apprehending a wanted criminal?"

"No, nothing as exciting as that," I sighed. "Pete wanted me to stop by on my way home, so he could tell me he won't be able to go this weekend."

"What's this weekend?"

"My endurance ride."

"That's right," Remy said, snapping his fingers. A frown darkened his face as he crammed his fists onto his hips. "Well, why the hell not!"

"According to Pete, he's being forced to attend his parents' 50th wedding anniversary back in Kentucky." I reached down and scooped up Bubbles as he trotted by. I reiterated my concerns about keeping Scott in line as I scratched the dog's ears.

"Uh-huh," Remy said, nodding his head. "Well, the way I see it, there's only one solution."

"Oh? And what is that?" I asked. Finished with the affection, Bubbles licked my face and squirmed out of my arms.

"Take me instead."

"Thanks for the offer Remy, but..."

"But what? I handled collecting Raven the other day just fine, didn't I?"

"Well sure, but we'll be camping out Friday night and coming home real late on Saturday. I don't think—that is, I mean..."

"What exactly do you mean?" Remy interrupted, crossing his arms in front of his chest as if daring me to answer.

At that point, I knew I was stuck. Anything I said would not be interpreted as my concern for his comfort but rather as a reflection of his age. I had no choice but to cave. "Fine. Will you be my support crew for the competition?"

"Darn tootin' I will!" he said, slapping the side of his leg. "That's what partners are for."

Good grief!

"Come on up and set a spell." He motioned toward the porch. "You can fill me in on what needs to be done ahead of time." Before I could reply, he hustled toward the house and disappeared through the front door.

I removed my gun belt and quickly stowed it in the Explorer before climbing the steps to the front porch and settling into one of the antique metal lawn chairs. Remy reappeared and offered me one of the two beers he was carrying. I started to refuse, ready to cite my training as to the reason, but the thought of that first sip of an ice-cold beer was more powerful than any willpower I could have mustered. I let him get comfortable and then said, "Other than having the tack ready, there really isn't too much to do. I was hoping to get together with Scott and Pete sometime Thursday just to go over how the competition goes and what to expect."

"Grand idea! Invite that Scott fella to my place, and I'll cook us some supper."

"Okay Remy," I chuckled. "What time do you want us here?"

"Let's shoot for five o'clock. That way there will be plenty of time for planning." We sat in silence for a few minutes, watching Bubbles and Millie romp around the yard before the conversation continued and in a different direction. "Got any new leads in your kidnapping case?" my self-appointed partner asked.

I explained about the discovery of the wild horse and how I had a gut feeling it was connected. "But until I find out who adopted it, I have no way of knowing for sure."

"What did that gal have to say about who grabbed her?"

"Not much. She claims she didn't get a chance to see what he looked like since he came up behind her and pulled a bag over her head. Apparently, he spoke to her, but she doesn't remember anything else until she regained consciousness the next day."

"Wonder if she'd recognize the guy's voice if she heard it again."

"I don't know. Maybe." I finished off the rest of my beer. "This whole thing has been one dead end after another."

"Well, you're welcome to stay for dinner if you like. Nothing fancy. Just some leftovers."

"Thanks, but after that snack you provided yesterday and this beer, I need to go home and work out." I stood and moved toward the steps.

"Alrighty then. See you in the morning."

I collected my dog and drove home. A few minutes later, I'd changed my clothes and was giving my sparring dummy a thorough beating, but my brain wouldn't let go of the investigation and allow me to focus on my workout. Finally, I gave up and jumped into the shower. Scrounging something to eat out of the fridge, I'd just plopped down on the couch to watch television when my cell phone began to ring. Unfortunately, I didn't get to it fast enough, and the call went to voice mail. As soon as I got the alert, I played the message.

"Hi Sarah, it's Bonnie. Sorry I'm calling after hours, but I just got a call about that mustang and thought you'd like the information. It was adopted about eight years ago by a Jonathan McGregor. Hope this helps."

Jonathan McGregor? That name didn't sound at all familiar. Another dead end. I snapped my phone shut and headed toward the kitchen, passing through my office on the way. Glancing at my desk, I subconsciously took inventory of the items scattered across it and halted in the doorway. Backing up, I looked again and, spotting the manilla envelope I'd left there a week ago, flashed on the comment Remy had made earlier. *Could Ida identify her attacker by listening to his voice?*

Statements given by the wranglers as well as the evidence, or rather the lack thereof, did not indicate that any of them were involved, but my instincts—*intuition?*—disagreed. And unless someone suddenly marched into the Sheriff's Office and confessed, having Ida listen to the recordings may be the only chance left of identifying, and thereby arresting, the kidnapper.

Chapter 19

With the manilla envelope tucked under my arm, I pushed through the reinforced glass door of the Sheriff's Office Wednesday morning, nodded at Cindy as I passed the dispatcher's desk and headed straight for the lab. I greeted the lanky technician who was seated at his desk, sipping his cup of morning coffee.

"Hey Sarah," he replied. "Whatcha got going on this morning?"

"I need to borrow that old tape recorder again."

"Sure thing. It's back in the cabinet. Help yourself."

"Thanks." I laid the envelope on the examination table and dug out the electronic relic.

"I hope you don't need any more tapes. I gave you my last one the other day."

"No, I'm good, thanks." As I exited the lab, my stomach informed me that the protein bar and cup of instant coffee I'd inhaled on my way over the pass was insufficient, so I headed for the break room and was not surprised to find Scott there choosing what I assumed would be his breakfast.

"Well, howdy Sarah," he said, retrieving his selection from the compartment at the bottom of the vending machine. "Heard you found your missing person."

"Yeah, I did but still no leads on who kidnapped her. At least not yet."

"Not yet?"

"Well, I had something kind of strange happen yesterday that I think is connected somehow, but I have to do some more investigating." I inserted money and punched in the combination for a bag of trail mix.

"Oh? What's that?"

"A rancher reported finding an extra horse on his property, and it just so happens to be a wild horse that was adopted a few years ago by a Jonathan McGregor. I need to find out if he's associated in any way with the group of wranglers that were at the round up."

Scott stopped chewing for a moment and began nodding his head. "I'm pretty sure that's the name of the last guy you wanted me to interview," he said after swallowing.

"No, the last guy you interviewed was named Nate."

"Nickname," he mumbled around his next bite of food.

I shook my head. "But the tape..."

"Yeah, about the tape." He flashed his stupid sheepish grin at me. "I'd forgotten to turn the recorder back on until after he'd said his name, and we talked about how my grandpa Jonathan had gone by the same nickname."

Unbelievable!

"So I stopped him, turned on the recorder and then had him start over answering the questions."

I couldn't decide whether to kiss Scott or punch him in the face but was leaning more toward the latter. However, with this new information, I had no time to do either. "Gotta go!" I said, gathering up my stuff, and headed for the hospital.

I knew it! I just knew it! Throughout this investigation my gut told me it was Nate, but I had no way to prove it. Now, all I had to do was have the victim identify her attacker's voice and issue an all-points bulletin in order to locate and arrest him.

I walked into Ida's room just as she was finishing her breakfast. "Good morning," I said, dropping my load on the end of her bed. "How are your feet?"

"Good. They're almost back to normal." Sitting up with her legs folded in front of her, she pushed the covers back far enough for one of her feet to show. The rash was almost gone as was most of the discoloration. "Doctor says I most likely will be discharged tomorrow," she said, pulling her bedding back into place. "I'll just have to have them checked in a week or so."

"That's great. I'll be sure to get your contact information before you leave town."

"Yeah, okay." She paused briefly as her expression darkened. "It's just..."

"Just what?"

"I don't have...that is, I've been..."

"You've been living in your car, haven't you?"

She nodded.

"And you really don't have anywhere to go?"

Her head slowly turned from side to side.

I knew that in some circumstances, the local district attorney had emergency funds for victims of crime, but I wasn't sure if Ida's situation would qualify. "Let me do some checking and see if there's any way we can help you."

"Oh, would you?" Her expression suddenly changed. "That would be wonderful!"

"Sure thing," I said. "But first, I may have discovered who kidnapped you."

"You have?"

"I believe so, but I need you to identify his voice. Think you can do that?"

"Absolutely!" She readjusted herself into a more upright position.

I removed her breakfast tray from the overbed table and balanced it on a nearby chair before placing the tape recorder in front of her and plugging it in. After removing the cassette from the envelope, I popped it into the recorder, B side up, pressed the rewind button for a few seconds and then hit play.

Scott's voice came out of the speaker, thanking the interviewee, followed by a few clunking sounds, indicating the stopping and starting again of the recording. "Okay, Nate..." Scott's voice. "...let's try this again."

Why didn't I notice that before?

Nate's voice poured from the speaker as he answered each of the scripted questions, and I stood quietly, giving Ida plenty of time to listen. As he neared the end, I asked, "Do you recognize his voice?"

"Sure do."

Yes! "So this is the voice of the man who kidnapped you?"

"No."

"What do you mean 'no'! You just said you recognized his voice."

"I do. It's that cowboy that yelled at me at the roundup. Not the guy that grabbed me at the gas station."

"Are you sure?"

"Positive. I told you, the kidnapper had a deep, chocolaty voice."

Chocolaty?

"Even though he said some really nasty things to me."

My instinct *(intuition?—ugh)* told me Nate was involved. What if he was the mastermind and had gotten someone else to do the dirty work? But who? If it was one of the wranglers he works with, maybe there was still a chance Ida might recognize his voice.

With that in mind, I flipped over the tape and rewound it to the beginning. One by one, we listened to the recorded interviews, fast-forwarding to the next one as soon as Ida shook her head.

Over an hour later, I still had no suspect, and it was becoming evident that Ida was bored with the activity. "Tell you what," I said, "I'll let you rest for a while, and I'll go get some lunch. This afternoon, I'll come back and play the rest of the interviews."

I left the hospital and drove straight to the Pitt for the second fast-food meal in a week and to contemplate whether or not I was wasting my time. My next challenge, however, was convincing Josh to loan me his tablet for an hour or two.

"Absolutely not!" Josh said, hugging his tablet to his chest. "All my stuff is on this thing."

"Oh, come on. You let me use it before."

"That's because you were using it right here in the office where I could keep an eye on it!"

"Then come with me," I suggested.

"No way!" he said, shaking his head. "Last time I had

to go into the field on one of your cases, I got covered in anaconda goo."

"Nothing like that is going to happen. I just need to have someone listen to the interviews I recorded," I said, holding up the flash drive he'd helped me save them to.

He shook his head again.

"Or…" I pulled the picture of Ida I'd clipped out of the paper and held it up. "…I can just bring her down here to your lab to listen."

Within seconds, he made his decision. "Fine, I'll come with you, but only for an hour and nothing weird or disgusting better happen."

"Relax. Piece of cake," I said, almost convincing myself.

Chapter 20

"This stew is delicious," Scott said, shoveling in another mouthful. "And this homemade bread," he added when he came up for air, "is perfect for soaking up the sauce."

"Are you even listening to me?" I demanded.

"Yeah, yeah, leave Friday from my place no later than one."

"That's right. Now, the next thing we need to discuss is sleeping arrangements. If we take my trailer, there is a small bed in the front for one of us, so the other two would have to sleep in the Dooley."

"Why don't we take my trailer? It's bigger, so we can put all our supplies in it rather than the bed of the truck. And we could do like we did in high school and bed down in it. It's definitely warm enough to do that."

"I don't know..." I glanced at Remy and then back at Scott. "Sleeping on the floor of the trailer isn't going to be very comfortable."

"What, are you getting soft in your old age?" Scott teased.

"Well, no it's just that..." I glanced at Remy again.

"She's afraid I'm too old for all that," he interrupted, crossing his arms in front of him and staring at me. "Aren't you?"

"No," I began, shaking my head.

He held up one hand. "Not that I need one, but I have some old army cots we can sleep on."

"Sounds good to me," Scott said, dishing himself a second bowl of stew. "So, you two will come over in the morning, hauling your horse in your trailer. Then we'll swap trailers, load up and go."

"That's the plan. We can grab burgers on the way out of town, but as far as dinner is concerned, campfires are not permitted, so we'll have to stop at a store and grab something on the way to base camp. The flyer says there will be light refreshments provided during the lunch stop, but we may want something after the race or on the way home."

"Don't you worry none about food," Remy said. "I'll take care of that. You just worry about what you gotta do for that there race."

"Thanks, Remy. That'll be a big help." I turned back to Scott. "How are you set for tack? You'll need a light saddle, helmet, and shoes that are comfortable and that you can run in. Oh, and you'll need something to carry water and snacks in."

"My cowboy hat is the only helmet I'll need, and I have an old training saddle that should work. As far as shoes go, I got work boots or cowboy boots, and the only saddlebags I have are for packing out animals that I use when I go hunting. I think I have a camo backpack that should work fine. Anything else?"

"Not for us," I said, trying to keep my voice as level as possible even though I was becoming increasingly more frustrated with Scott and his make-do attitude. "We will need hay for the horses as well as apples and carrots for them to eat on the trail. I'll throw in a container of oats, and we'll also need something to put water in for them out on the trail."

"That's where the cowboy hat comes in," Scott said, winking at me. "Shade for me and a watering trough for my horse. As far as hay goes, I've got a nice bale of grass we can throw in."

"No need to worry about those apples and carrots either," Remy offered. "I've got a big batch of them for Millie. And..." The timer on the stove interrupted him. "Oh, hang on a second." He got up from the table, slipped on a large oven mitt, and pulled a baking sheet out of the oven.

"Hey, those smell delicious," Scott said, joining him in the kitchen. "But aren't those supposed to flatten out when they bake?"

"Don't know. Never made 'em before."

Curious to see what they were talking about, I moved over to where Remy was taking something resembling large, dark pellets off the baking sheet and placing them on a cooling rack. Without hesitating, Scott plucked one off the rack and popped it into his mouth.

"Here, now!" Remy scolded. "What do you think you are doing?"

"Just having a sample of dessert," Scott said around the mouthful. "Kinda dry though, got any milk?"

"For your information, young fella, that ain't dessert. Them there are horse cookies I'm baking to take with us."

He stopped chewing and stared at my neighbor. "Horse cookies?"

"Yup. Shellie found the recipe for me on her computer. Made out of carrots, flour, oats, and molasses."

Scott chewed a couple more times and then swallowed. "Not bad."

"Well, you just stay out of them." Remy placed the baking sheet in the sink and took off the oven mitt. "Say, did you ever find out who that wild horse belonged to?" he asked, directing the question at me.

"Yeah," I replied.

"Belongs to one of the wranglers we interviewed," Scott added, eyeing the horse cookies.

Before he could sample another one, Remy guided us into the living room. "So, then it is connected to the kidnapping of that gal."

"Yes...no...I mean...oh, I don't know." I flopped down on one end of the couch. "I really thought I had my kidnapper, but when I played the recording of his interview for her, she claimed it wasn't the guy who grabbed her. Which kind of makes sense because the horse he was riding the day of the roundup was a big sorrel, and this mustang is smaller, dark brown, and has a black mane and tail. Maybe he was riding someone else's horse. And why would he leave his horse behind?" Sensing the start of a tension headache, I closed my eyes and pinched the bridge of my nose.

"Did you play the rest of the interviews for her?" Remy asked. "Maybe it was another one of them fellas."

"Of course I did!" I snapped and immediately regretted it. "Sorry." I shrugged. "It's just that this whole thing has been very frustrating."

Scott stretched his legs out in front of him and laced his fingers behind his head. "And then there's those articles in the newspaper."

"Ugh," I moaned. "The damn articles!"

"Articles?" Remy snagged his paper off the coffee table. "What articles? I haven't had a chance to look at this yet." He unfolded the periodical and began thumbing through the pages. "Here's one." He folded the page back and began reading. "Kidnap victim, Ida Dudley, was rescued last Sunday from a remote location in Nevada by Deputy Sarah Murdock." He stopped reading. "Nothing wrong with that," he said.

"Keep going," I said.

He continued reading about how I had happened to find Ida, how I gave her food before riding back to get help, and how we rescued her by helicopter. "This all sounds great. What's the big deal?"

I rotated the fingers of my right hand, indicating that he continue.

"'The thing I don't understand,' Dudley said, 'is why she left me behind, even when I begged her not to. She told me herself that no one knew where I was, but when she tricked me, so she could ride off without me, I was terrified.'" Remy stopped reading again. "Oh."

"I was hoping she wouldn't say anything about that, considering I came back and rescued her, but there it is in black and white for all to see."

"I'm guessing the sheriff saw it, and that's why you were in his office," Scott said.

"Yeah, but once I explained the situation, he agreed I took the correct course of action." I stood and stretched before grabbing a handful of dirty dishes and taking them into the kitchen. "At least, Sandusky is gone, or he would've most likely chewed my ass up one side and down the other about how the Sheriff's Office doesn't need that kind of bad publicity...blah, blah, blah."

"Well, good thing there wasn't a picture with it," Remy said, refolding the paper.

"Next section," Scott instructed, "third or fourth page in."

Remy easily spotted the picture of Ida sitting in her hospital bed and read the headline, "Courageous Battle to Save Wild Horses." He paused again. "Who the hell wrote this stuff?"

"Lulu DeLoure," I said, taking the nearly empty pot of stew into the kitchen.

"Isn't she that crazy reporter with the pink hair?" he asked. "How did she get involved?"

"I invited her to interview Ida," I admitted.

"What in tarnation did you do that for?" Remy said, hastily folding the paper and tossing it back onto the coffee table.

"It's a long story," I replied. "Where would you like me to put these horse cookies?"

Remy left his chair and joined me in the kitchen. "Here, I'll bag 'em up. You, young fella," he called to Scott, who hadn't moved a muscle to help, "clear off the rest of the table, and we'll have this mess cleaned up in no time."

"Oh, sure thing," Scott scrambled to his feet.

"Anyway," Remy continued, "once she's out of the hospital, you'll be done with her, won't you?"

"Not yet," I said, shaking my head. "Because she's technically homeless, and because she has to be given one final medical check next week, and because she is the only way to identify any potential suspects, Cindy contacted the district attorney's office and made arrangements for her to stay at the Stoney Ridge Motor Lodge for the next two weeks." I took the last of the dirty dishes from Scott and submerged them in the hot, soapy water I'd run in the sink. "In fact, someone should've helped her retrieve her car and get settled in her motel room today."

"All the more reason to put the whole thing outta your head and focus on your ride."

"He's right, Sarah," Scott chimed in. "It's not like she's still missing."

"That's true," I admitted.

"And if I know you, you've followed every possible lead there was," he added, "but sometimes you just have to give up."

But I don't have to like it! "Fine. As of right now, the only thing on my mind is getting to the competition and riding."

"That's my partner," Remy said.

Scott leaned in closer. "Partner?" he whispered.

"Never mind," I said, positioning him in front of the sink, "just start washing."

Within a few minutes, Remy had the food put away, and we had all the dishes washed and dried. Scott leaned against the counter with his arms crossed over his chest. "Now what?"

"I think we're set to go," I said.

"Good, because I have some things I need to get done tonight," Remy said as he ushered us toward the front door.

"Can I help with anything?" I asked.

"Nope. Don't need nobody getting in the way. You two just get on home and do what you gotta do, and I'll see you tomorrow." Before I had a chance to say anything else, he pushed us out the door and closed it.

"Well goodnight, Sarah," Scott called as he headed for his GMC pickup.

"Night." As I drove the short distance back to my place, I wondered just how successful this weekend was going to be.

Chapter 21

When I pulled into Remy's driveway midmorning, it was quite obvious he was ready to go. Three wooden cots were piled at the bottom of the front steps and an ice chest, sleeping bag, and a small khaki duffel bag were stacked at the top. Remy, himself, was sitting in the middle of the steps, and before I could come to a complete stop, he was on his feet and hauling stuff toward the truck.

"Good morning," he said as he hefted two of the cots into the bed of the Dooley.

"Morning, Remy," I replied, having jumped out and moved around the front of the truck, Bubbles at my heels. "Let me help you with the rest of your gear."

"Thanks. I think it will take both of us to load that cold box."

I grabbed the duffel and sleeping bag, tossed them in the backseat, and dropped the tailgate. Then I went back to help move the ice chest. "What on earth do you have in here? It weighs a ton."

"Just the rations we'll need is all." I knew from the grin on his face, it was more than that.

"So Remy," I said after we struggled to get the ice chest onto the tailgate, "I was wondering if I could leave

Bubbles here with Millie. I really don't have a place to leave him at home."

"Here?"

"Well...yeah." I motioned toward the old chicken coop where Remy had put Millie when I first brought her to his place. "Aren't you going to leave her in there?"

"Nope."

"Where are you leaving her?"

"I ain't. Figured she'd enjoy going on an adventure. Besides, she hasn't spent the night away from me since I got her. Has Bubbles?"

"Has Bubbles what?"

"Spent the night away from you since you got him?"

"Well no, but I don't think the two of them should be running around at the competition."

"Who says they'll be running around." He let out a loud whistle and Millie and Bubbles ran over to him. Then he held out his right hand with his palm facing them, and both animals lowered their haunches to the ground. "See there. They're quite well-behaved."

Again, I questioned the success of the weekend. "But you have to promise to keep them with you at all times."

"You betcha," Remy said, opening the back door of the truck and signaling the two animals to get inside. "You got food for Bubba?" he asked after closing the door.

"Yes, I brought some because I thought I was leaving him here."

"Then we're all set." Without another word, he climbed into the passenger seat.

"Yeah...all set."

After a quick stop at Rabbit Traxx to top off the fuel tank, we arrived at Scott's an hour later. I pulled alongside his livestock trailer in order to make the switch as easy as possible. "While I unhook, I'd appreciate it if you'd unload Raven and tie him up next to Raz on the other side of Scott's trailer," I said to Remy.

"Will do."

I'd just backed into position in front of Scott's trailer when he appeared pushing a wheelbarrow loaded with a large bale of hay and wearing a sweat-stained Resistol hat with a tight weave crown. The sides were curled up, and the front of the brim was pulled down so far I was surprised he could see where he was going.

"I'll dump this in the end of the trailer. That way we won't have to bust a gut trying to get it into the bed of the truck."

Staring at the tattered cowboy hat I replied, "Sounds good to me. Hey, guide me in will you?"

"You got it." He abandoned the wheelbarrow and slid in between the truck and trailer, and with only a couple of slight adjustments, we had it connected.

"So, is that the hat you were talking about?" I asked.

"Yup." He pulled it off and spun it around a couple of times. "Isn't it a beaut?"

I wanted to shake my head—shake it vigorously, but all I could do was nod—slowly.

Scott crammed the hat back on his head. "I'll go get my saddle," he called over his shoulder as he pushed the empty wheelbarrow back toward the small metal shed he used for a tack room.

Remy and I transferred the portable corral panels from my trailer to Scott's and secured them with a few of my cinch straps. I packed the rest to hold the panels together once we reached camp.

"We ready to put them horses inside?" Remy asked.

"Yes, they'll need to go in before we can get the tack loaded," I replied, "but I'm not sure how Raz is going to act." Even though I'd been around the horse for awhile, I'd never seen him load into a trailer, and Scott had not yet returned. "You hold onto Raven, and I'll take Raz in first. Then you can bring him over."

"Alrighty then." Remy untied my horse and led him around in a circle while I attempted to load Scott's Arabian. Getting him to the back of the trailer was no problem, but when I stepped inside, he balked and then reared up slightly, pawing at the air with his front legs like a toddler throwing a tantrum.

As I tried again to coax the horse into the trailer, Scott appeared, carrying his saddle. "Raz! Hup!"

To my amazement, the horse stopped pulling back on the lead rope and practically leapt into the trailer. I quickly moved him into position and tied the lead rope to a D-ring with a quick release safety knot. "How did you train him to do that?" I asked Scott as I stepped out of the trailer.

He dumped his saddle onto the hay bale. "Old rancher's trick. Make being outside the trailer more uncomfortable than inside. Hook that to a command, and it works every time."

"As long as you know the magic word, it does." I took Raven's lead rope, and the gelding obediently followed me inside. "Now that the horses are loaded," I said, after tying him next to Raz, "I'll get my tack moved over, and we can get going."

"Sounds good," Scott said. "I'll grab the rest of mine,

too. The only other things I have are my bedroll and bag, which are sitting by the door."

"I'll fetch 'em for you," Remy offered.

"Yeah, thanks."

Not wanting to forget anything essential, I pictured my last endurance ride in my mind and mentally ticked off each step, selecting the tack and equipment I'd need. By the time I had everything loaded and my trailer locked up, the guys were back.

Scott tossed his tack into the trailer, where it lay in a tangled heap. "Here, I'll take that," he said to Remy, relieving the older gentleman of the items he was holding. "I'll just put them in here." He jerked open the back door on the driver's side but jumped back when Millie and Bubbles tumbled out. "What the heck! What are these two doing here?" He placed his stuff on the seat and slammed the door.

"They're just along for the ride," Remy informed him.

"No way! Don't need them getting underfoot around the horses."

"Either they go or I don't."

"Fine by me. Don't know why we had to have some old guy tagging along anyway."

Unbelievable! "That's enough Scott," I began, but Remy's raised hand made me stop.

"Fine," he said, "just unload my cots."

"Fine." Scott reached into the bed of the Dooley and pulled them out.

"And unload that cold box of mine, too, while you're at it," Remy added, folding his arms across his chest and rocking back on his heels. That's when I understood.

"The ice chest?" Scott exclaimed. He looked at me; I assumed hoping for backup, but I just stood quietly and tried not to smile.

"Come on, you can't be serious," Scott continued. "What are we supposed to eat?"

"Well, either we all go," Remy said, nodding toward the animals, "or nothin' of mine goes."

For the longest time, Scott just stood there staring at Remy. "Fine," he said at last and put the cots back into the bed of the truck. "But I'm calling shotgun. No way am I riding in the back with a goat."

"Suits me just fine." Remy climbed into the backseat and was immediately joined by Millie and Bubbles. "And," he continued when Scott and I got in, "the way I see it, you're treating to burgers on the way out of town."

"Yeah, yeah. Fine," Scott grumbled.

What have I gotten myself into?

"First thing we'll need to do is put up the panels, so we can unload the horses and give them some hay and water," I said as I navigated down the narrow dirt road.

"I'll be happy to help as soon as I take a piss," Scott said.

"Uh-uh, you know the rule, Scott Jenkins."

The man in the passenger seat sighed. "Horses before humans," he murmured.

"That's right. Now, watch for a good place to park."

A mile off the main road, we reached base camp where at least ten rigs had already pulled in and set up. "This side looks pretty full," Scott said, pointing to the right. A couple of rigs had parked in the triangle of land between the two forks of the road, but I didn't think there would be enough room for the portable corral.

"Why don't we swing around and park along that there other road? That way we're already headed out when this is over," Remy suggested.

"That's a good idea." I continued to follow the road on the right until it opened up in the center of camp. Veering left, I slowly pulled around the triangle of land.

"Be right there," Scott said as he suddenly opened his door and bailed out. He ran across camp toward a small trailer carrying two portable outhouses.

I rolled down his window and called after him. "Don't make me wait on you!" The only response I got was a hand wave just before he disappeared into one of them.

"Ugh. Sometimes that man..."

"Seems to me," Remy interjected, "he can be a might annoying."

At least it isn't just me! "Yes, Remy he can. It's like rules are for everyone else, and he's not afraid of any consequences." I completed the turn and pulled off in a nice wide area with only a few scattered sagebrush. "The only consequences he ever feared came from Chet Atkins."

"The country-western singer?"

I laughed and shook my head. "No, Sheriff Atkins. His solution to Scott's rebel-like behavior has been to have him chauffeur dead bodies to Redding, usually after he's worked a full shift." I shut down the engine, and we got out. "Keep an eye on those two, would you, and I'll get started on the corral, so we can unload the horses."

"Will do," Remy said as he opened the door and freed the two small animals. He led them away from camp, so they could romp and take care of any pending biological needs.

By the time I got to the back of the trailer, Scott was already there and releasing the door latches. "Told ya I'd be right here," he said through that crooked smile of his.

"Yeah, yeah. Now help me get these panels out and in place." Seeming to emphasize the urgency, Raven stomped and let out a low chuckle.

As soon as we had the horses turned out in the make-shift corral, I ushered Millie and Bubbles into the trailer, relieving Remy of his obligation. "Feel free to stretch your legs and have a look around. Scott and I need to feed and water the horses and then take them over for their initial vet check."

"Okay, be back in a jiffy."

While Remy was exploring, Scott and I stuffed the hay net and filled the water bucket I'd brought. "Might as well unload the ice chest and bring the cots inside the trailer," I suggested.

"Sure thing," Scott replied.

After lugging the ice chest together, I double-checked the schedule on the packet of information I'd printed out, and Scott finished moving the cots. Just as I closed the door of the Dooley, I heard shouting; it was Remy. I dashed around the front of my truck and found him standing by the trailer's escape door.

"Why in tarnation are you setting up our beds over piles of horse turds?" he demanded.

"Relax," Scott said. "It's no big deal. Just don't walk around in your socks."

"Unacceptable!" Remy countered. "Get them cots outta there, right now!"

"Oh man, try doing something nice for somebody…" Scott grabbed the cot he'd just set up and shoved it out the door. I quickly grabbed the other two, which were still folded up, and carried them outside.

"Come on, Scott" I said, ushering him away from Remy and toward the registration area. "We need to check in, get our rider cards and take the horses for their pre-ride vet check." As we walked away, I could hear Remy muttering to himself as he banged things around inside the trailer.

"Hold up for a second," I told Scott when we passed by the trailer with the outhouses. "My turn." I rejoined him a few minutes later, and we moved over to the sign-in table, which was located under a large pop-up canopy.

I gave the guy sitting behind the sign for the 30-mile ride our names, and he handed over our rider packets. "Vet check is at the end of the pens," he said, nodding over his left shoulder, "and the rider meeting is here at seven o'clock."

"Great, thanks." I passed over Scott's packet "The most important thing in here is your rider card." I opened my own envelope and pulled out mine. "You have to show this at each vet check, so make sure it goes in your pocket or backpack. There should also be a map outlining each of the loops in there, which you'll want to take to the meeting later."

"Got it."

I glanced over at the vet area. "The line isn't too bad, so let's go get the horses and get their pre-ride check done."

"I'm up for anything that keeps some distance between me and that cantankerous old man."

"Oh come on, Scott. He's really not such a bad guy.
You just seem to be rubbing him the wrong way today."

"Well, why does he have to make things so damn
complicated?"

"He's not." I sighed. "He just has his own way of doing
things."

When we got back to the trailer, Bubbles and Millie
were still inside, but Remy was gone. Scott seemed relieved, but I was a little concerned because I couldn't see
him anywhere.

"Come on,"Scott said as he hooked up Raz's lead rope,
"I'm sure he's around here somewhere." While I removed
the cinch straps and made an opening in the corral, he
secured my horse as well, and we started for the vet area.

Chapter 22

As we made our way across camp, Raven plodded along behind me as if we were merely going for a stroll. Scott's horse, on the other hand, had his ears twitching and nostrils flaring as his head turned first one direction and then another. In fact, he was so distracted, I was surprised that he didn't plow right over the top of Scott as he led him along.

"When we get in line, keep a good hold on your horse," I said. "Don't let him sniff noses with other horses."

"Why not?" He stared at me for a few seconds, and then the crooked smile appeared. "Wait ... you jerking my chain?"

"No."

"Then why not?"

"Well ... it's considered rude."

"Jeez," Scott muttered. "This is going to be a very long weekend." The way things were going, I couldn't argue with that.

Getting into line, I became aware of some kind of commotion going on behind us. I turned around just in time to see the numerous people, who had been quietly leading their horses to one place or another, scattering in all directions, trying to clear a path for a large motor home towing a huge horse trailer. It crept through the center of camp, attempting to negotiate the same left-hand turn we had made earlier.

"Oh man, I don't think it's going to make it," Scott said.

"It will definitely be close, if it does."

Slowly, the leviathan of a vehicle inched closer and closer to the portable outhouse trailer. My body tensed in anticipation of a collision, and it seemed time stood still as everyone watched and waited. But nothing happened. With inches to spare, the motor home cleared the small trailer, and we all sighed in unison.

"So much for a little excitement." Scott sounded genuinely disappointed. "I can't believe anyone would drive something like that on anything other than pavement."

I had to agree. Most of the rigs parked around camp included trucks and livestock trailers with built-in living quarters. A handful of groups were roughing it like us, sleeping in their trailers or in tents they had pitched nearby. "They must really ..."

"Sarah? Sarah Murdock?"

Where is that voice coming from? I looked around but didn't recognize anyone.

"Over here."

I looked around again and this time spotted someone waving at me. Tossing Raven's lead rope to Scott, I headed for the end of the line that had grown behind us. As soon as the woman smiled, I knew who she was. "Bernie Saunders, what a pleasant surprise! I haven't seen you in ages."

"It's been at least two years," she said as we shared a hug.

"I'm glad to see you're still competing. This is my first one since relocating to California."

"You moved?" She laughed. "Me, too—Idaho."

I heard Scott's whistle. Glancing in his direction, I could see our turn was coming up. "Well, I have to go," I said, pointing back the way I'd come. "I'll watch for you at the meeting later."

"Sounds good."

I jogged back to the vet area and got there just as they were waving Scott over. I'd planned on giving him a quick rundown of what to expect but didn't get the chance.

He handed over his rider card, and one of the assistants wrote his number on Raz's rump with a black grease crayon. While the control judge lifted Raz's lip and pressed on his gums, Scott looked at me and shrugged his shoulders slightly. While the pressing of her thumb on the horse's neck, the pinching of skin over the shoulder, and listening for heart rate and gut sounds got no reaction from him, when she started checking for muscle and anal tone, which involves palpating, poking and prodding of the horse's rear end, Scott's head whipped around, and he looked at me with such a hilarious expression of surprise and disgust, I had to bite my lower lip to keep from laughing. When the judge asked him to trot Raz out and back, I hoped he had an appropriate command for that because it's harder than it looks. However, I was waved over at that moment and didn't get to watch.

Raven passed his pre-ride vet check with straight As, which was better than I expected. Pleased with his score, I anticipated a good run in the competition, but more than that, I was looking forward to spending time alone with my horse.

I waved at Bernie as I left the vet area and headed back to the trailer. Scott was reclining on one of the fenders with his legs stretched out in front of him and his arms folded across his chest. As I got closer, I could see his eyes were closed, too.

"Hey," I said, kicking one of his feet.

His body lurched, and his eyes popped open. "Huh?" he said, looking around. "Oh, hi."

Just the reaction I was looking for! "So how did Raz do on his vet check?"

"Got better grades than I ever did." He stood and pulled his rider card out of his hip pocket. "Most things got an A or A-, but I had a real hard time getting him to trot along beside me, so he got a B- on gait, impulsion, and attitude. I think there was just too much going on." He replaced his card and opened the corral, so I could lead Raven inside.

"He did seem distracted, but it looks like he's quieted down some," I said, watching the Arabian nibble at a few stalks of hay that had collected on the ground. "Here." I handed him the hay net. "We need to reload this and feed them some oats as well. You'll find the container in the bed of the truck and a bucket to feed with."

"Got it."

"And have you seen Remy?" I asked. Scott gestured toward the other side of the trailer. "Okay. I'll go check on him if you'll take care of the horses."

"Sure thing."

Walking around the front of my truck, I spotted Millie

and Bubbles chasing each other through the nearby sagebrush. "Remy?"

"Right here," he answered as he emerged from the trailer. "How did it go?"

"Good. After the rider meeting, we should be all set to go."

"And when is that?" he asked.

"Seven."

"Well then, I 'spect I should lay us out some dinner." He climbed back into the trailer, and I stepped in behind him.

"Why Remy, what have you done in here?" The floor had been swept clean of any equine excrement and replaced with a nice layer of sawdust. Each of the three cots had been set up and designated by the belongings it held.

"Oh, just a little housekeeping." He opened the ice chest and began pulling out containers, including a gallon jug filled with a brown liquid. Then he pulled out a few paper plates and a bag of plastic utensils. After he had removed everything he wanted, he closed the ice chest and began arranging things on top. "I have a lantern for later when it gets dark, but it's not real bright."

"Hold on. I might have a flashlight in the truck." Not certain where it was, I started searching the glove box then the center console and finally found it behind the back seat. Even better, it lit up when I pushed the button.

I'd just demonstrated that to Remy when Scott stuck his head in. "Wow, just look at this place."

"A might better than tiptoeing through turds, ain't it?" Remy said. "Now, come on in and get something to eat," he continued before Scott had a chance to say anything.

"I brought honey-roasted short ribs, baked beans, macaroni salad, and deviled eggs." He handed each of us a plate and began opening the containers. The smell coming from each one was wonderful, and I'm fairly certain I heard Scott's stomach growl. "There's sweet tea to wash it all down and for dessert, strawberry rhubarb hand pies."

"Wow. This all looks so good," Scott said. "I'm starving!" He dug a fork out of the bag of utensils and reached for a rib.

Remy stepped over to the escape door and whistled. "Still don't know why you gotta have some old guy tag along?" he asked.

Scott stopped mid-reach and straightened up. "Look," he began, "I'm really sorry, for giving you such a hard time. It's just ..."

Before he could finish, Millie and Bubbles leapt inside the trailer and began jumping on and off the cots. "Here now," Remy scolded. "Simmer down you two." He gave them the same hand signal he'd used in his driveway, and both animals immediately halted and sat in place. "As for you ..." He turned his attention back to Scott. "...apology accepted. Now dig in!"

I could tell from the expression on Remy's face that he felt triumphant, which he was, hitting Scott where it hurts the most—his stomach.

Relieved that the conflict was over, I filled my own plate and enjoyed every bite.

Chapter 23

"There she is," I said, pointing to my friend and two other women who were standing off to the side of the main crowd that had gathered in the registration area. Most had brought some kind of folding chair; the rest stood along the fringes.

"Hey Sarah," Bernie called when she noticed us. "I saved you a spot." I waved an acknowledgement, and we weaved our way over to them.

"This is Louise Tyke and Charlene Smith," Bernie said, gesturing toward her companions. "Girls, this is Sarah Murdock."

We exchanged pleasantries, and I introduced Scott. "So, how long have you been doing these rides?" he asked.

"I've been competing for 30 years." Louise's leathery skin and deep tan validated her statement.

"Really? I had no idea it had been around that long," he said.

"Sure has."

"And she recently reached her 10,000 mile mark too," Charlene added.

"I did a lot of riding in my sixties after I retired. But Charlene here is no slacker."

"I have just over 3,000 myself," she said, "but I've only been riding about ten years."

"Wow!" I looked at Bernie. "I've been riding for five years, and I'm not even sure I've reached 1,000 miles."

"Same here," she chuckled. "Guess now we've got something to shoot for."

"And how about you?" Louise asked Scott. "This your first time competing?"

"Yeah, how did you know?"

The two veteran riders exchanged a covert glance. "Oh, lucky guess."

"Now stop it, Louise," Charlene scolded. "Actually, we were over by the vet check area when you went through. It was pretty obvious it was your first time."

Scott looked at me, and I gave him a slight nod.

"But that's okay," Charlene continued. "We seem to have several newbies this time. In fact, the sweetest old gentleman came by, looking for a shovel or broom he could borrow. He told us this was his first time at one of these competitions, too"

"At first, he seemed a little upset," Louise said. "Seems whoever he's with wasn't concerned with cleaning out the trailer before setting up their beds."

I turned toward Scott, but he appeared to be intently inspecting his shoes.

"I even gave him a partial bag of sawdust to put down," Charlene said.

I smiled. "That would've been our support crew, Remy. He and Scott seemed to have different ideas on what was acceptable, so thanks for helping him out."

"Oh, it was our pleasure," Louise said.

"And besides," Charlene added, "he brought us a couple of delicious turnovers when he brought the tools back."

Sounds like Remy! "So Bernie, are you riding the 30-mile or the 50?"

"These two have convinced me to ride the 50."

"The 50-mile is easier," Louise said.

Charlene shook her head. "I wouldn't necessarily say that it's easier, but if I'm going to go to all the trouble to haul my horse out here, I'm going to spend as much time in the saddle as possible." All nodded in agreement.

Conversations throughout the crowd began to diminish as three women left the registration table and moved to the front. The tallest of the three, clipboard in hand, stepped forward. "Before we get started, I'd like to introduce the head control judge, Dr. Suzanne Tanner; our head timer, Betty Bison; and I'm Margo Barnett, this year's ride manager." A short round of applause followed. "First off, I'd like to thank you all for competing this year. I think you'll find each loop is a great ride. I'd also like to thank the local ranchers for helping us provide plenty of water in several locations for our horses."

She paused and reviewed her notes before continuing. "This year's 50 includes a 20-mile loop, which takes you east toward Moon Rocks and is almost entirely cross-country. We have it well-marked with yellow ribbons.

"The other two loops for this ride are what make up the 30-mile ride as well. The pink loop provides some great hill work, especially at the upper end, and the majority of this loop follows a narrow jeep track. The blue loop gives you the most variety and includes wide dirt roads, jeep tracks, and single-track trails. Keep your eyes open for the local wildlife. We've seen coyotes, deer, and occasional antelope, and even a few wild horses out there."

Oh great, more wild horses!

"We've tried to stagger the hold times to avoid big crowds at the vet check, and there will be a separate pulse area when you first arrive at each hold—all of which are back here at base camp.

"Our drag riders this year include members of the local search and rescue group as well as veteran endurance riders. They all will have radios, first-aid kits, water, aspirin, and have been trained in equine first-aid. Their horses have a triangular shaped symbol on their rumps instead of a number, so they'll be easy to spot. Are there any questions?"

Murmurs passed through the crowd until, finally, an older man toward the back raised his hand. "There was something mentioned about snacks being provided."

"Oh yeah, thanks. We have deli trays, rolls, and chips we'll put out about the time riders are coming in for the first holds. There will also be hay and plenty of water available for humans and horses. And remember to take lots of snacks and water out on the trail for yourself as well as your horse."

Betty Bison, the antithesis of her name with her small, slight build and blond hair, stepped over to Margo and whispered in her ear.

"And our head timer would like to remind you to call out your number each time you enter and leave the hold. It just helps our timers keep track." She glanced at the others still sitting at the registration table. "Anything else to mention?"

"Starting times?" someone in the crowd called out.

Margo laughed. "Oh that would be helpful, wouldn't it? The 50s start at seven o'clock tomorrow morning, and the 30s start at eight. So go get some rest, and if you're anything like me, good luck falling asleep." People chuckled in agreement as they began to disperse.

"Well, see you sometime tomorrow," I said to Bernie before she and her friends started back to their rigs. "Have a safe ride."

"Thanks, you too."

"I think we should go over our tack and make sure everything is in order," I suggested as Scott and I headed back to the trailer. "There won't be a lot of time to do it in the morning."

"Sure thing," he replied. "There's nothing else to do before hitting the hay."

No one, man nor beast, was at the trailer when we got back, so we began preparing our gear. I had mine checked and ready to go and my saddlebags packed, before Scott had finished untangling the mess he'd tossed into the trailer before we left. Anxious to be done, I gave him a hand, and we finished just as Remy and his furry companions returned.

"Where have you been?" Scott asked.

"Just out for an evening constitutional." He surveyed our progress. "Looks like you're all set."

"I think so. Scott here still needs to load his backpack. There's bottled water in the bed of the truck," I told him.

"Did you find the snacks?" Remy asked.

"No," I replied, "hadn't gotten that far."

"Let me fetch 'em." He soon returned with reclosable plastic bags. Two for each of us with apples and carrots in one and his freshly baked horse cookies in the other. "Now remember," he said as he handed Scott his, "these here cookies are for the horse, not you."

"Gotcha." Scott stuffed the bags of snacks in his backpack. I, however, took a little more time being careful to balance the weight between the two saddlebags.

Suddenly, I was very tired. "Well, I think I'm going to turn in. Pretty strenuous day tomorrow."

"Eh, nothing but a timed trail ride," Scott said through his crooked smile.

"We'll see," I told him. *We'll see.*

As tired as I was, I couldn't fall asleep. The other two seemed to drop off within minutes of going to bed, but I lay on my back staring into the darkness and listening to the rattle of nearby generators for a long time. It wasn't until they shut down one by one, leaving only silence behind, did I finally drift off to sleep.

Chapter 24

I woke to the sound of preparations being made for a day of riding and the smell of coffee. *Where is that coming from?* Remy's cot was empty and loud snoring came from the heap on Scott's. Taking advantage of being alone, so to speak, I quickly changed into my knee-length compressions shorts and a loose T-shirt as well as clean socks and my cross-trainers. Then I rebraided my hair, located my sunglasses and slid them onto the top of my head. Ready to go, I gave Scott's cot a solid kick. "Hey, time to get up!"

A groan from the heap was the only reply.

"Come on, we got stuff to do."

"Yeah, yeah," he mumbled into the covers. "I'm coming."

I hopped down from the trailer into the light of pre-dawn and stretched my stiff muscles. After loosening up a bit, I refilled the hay net and gave each horse a generous serving of oats. As the sun peeked over the distant mountain range, I extended my arms, closed my eyes, and soaked up the morning's first rays.

"Don't you have nothing better to do than stand around?" It was Remy—and he had coffee!

"Where did you find this?" I asked as he handed me

one of the three small styrofoam cups filled with the treasured liquid.

"Oh, I've got my sources." He continued toward the trailer. "Guess I better set out breakfast."

I followed him inside and wasn't too surprised to find Scott still in his socks and boxers, sitting on his cot.

"Don'tcha think it's time you was getting dressed?" Remy asked, handing him one of the remaining cups of coffee.

"I'm working on it," Scott replied.

Remy opened the ice chest and pulled out two large, reclosable plastic bags and set them on top of the closed lid. "I've got a breakfast casserole cut into squares for easy eating and some maple oatmeal muffins."

"Sounds delicious," Scott said as he reached for a muffin.

"Uh-uh, young fella," Remy said. "Not until you got some clothes on."

As Scott got dressed in jeans, a wife beater undershirt and a sleeveless, green plaid western shirt which he left unbuttoned, I helped myself to a large square of casserole. Even though it was cold, the combination of sausage, onion and bell pepper surrounded by the cooked eggs was perfect.

Scott had scarcely stomped into his work boots before grabbing his own piece of casserole with his right hand and a muffin with his left. "Oh man, these are good," he said in between alternating bites. "I didn't realize I was so hungry."

"Must be all this fresh air," I offered, selecting my own muffin. It, like the casserole, was delicious but very filling. I was stuffed by the time I had finished it.

Scott, on the other hand, had seconds of both. But when he reached for a third muffin, I stopped him. "Don't eat so much," I warned. "It might not stay down."

He sat on his cot for a minute as if analyzing what I'd said. "You're right." Then he took two more and stuffed them into the outside pocket of his backpack. "For later."

I finished off the last of my coffee and went outside to begin my own preparations for the ride. First, I brushed Raven from nose to tail, making sure there was nothing that could become an irritant under his saddle. Then I cleaned out each hoof and checked to make sure all four shoes were securely attached. The grooming done, I carefully positioned the pad and saddle and tightened the cinch. By the time I tied the saddlebags into place, the five minute warning for the start of the 50-mile race was announced, so I walked down to the gate.

Many of the horses could have been clones of Scott's white Arabian, but there were several other breeds in a variety of colors and ranging from ponies to even a small draft horse. Some groups were families with members of all ages. Helmet cameras were perched on the heads of at least half the riders, and others had small cameras mounted on the ends of long poles. Milling about as they waited to start, riders wished each other good luck and took selfies with their smart phones. The air was charged with the growing excitement.

I spotted Bernie with Louise and Charlene just as the head timer opened the gate, so even though I didn't get to talk to them, I waved as they headed out onto the trail.

Anxious to get started on my own ride, I headed back toward the trailer. Most of the horses I passed, either tethered to the sides of trailers or in their own portable corrals, were moving back and forth with anticipation and occasionally whinnying to each other. Even our own horses were wound up enough that Scott was having difficulty saddling Raz. Trying to help, I bridled my horse as quickly as I could and led him out of the corral, securing it behind us.

"I'm going to start warming up Raven and would suggest you do the same as soon as you're ready. It should calm him down some." I lowered my sunglasses into place and dug out my helmet.

"Gotcha," Scott replied, continuing to wrestle with his horse.

Turning away before he saw the huge grin on my face, I pulled on my helmet and guided the black gelding down the road we drove in on and urged him into a slow trot. The way he tossed and shook his head told me he wanted to go faster, but I kept his pace in check. About ten minutes later, we reached the cattle guard that stretched across the dirt road and turned around. Continuing to keep him at a slow trot, we returned to base camp.

I'd just spotted Scott walking Raz in a large circle when the head timer announced the fifteen minute warning for the 30-mile ride. "All warmed up?" I asked as I approached them and rode along.

"Working on it," Scott replied. "He's in spaz mode. I just now got him to stop crow hopping and listen to what I'm trying to tell him."

"Why don't you trot out that way ..." I pointed back the way I'd come. "... for about five minutes and then turn around and trot back. That should finish warming him up just before they open the gate."

"Good idea." He spun his horse around and started down the road.

I went in the opposite direction back to the trailer to do one last inspection. That done, I left Raven tied to the side of the trailer and headed for the rustic facilities. On the way there, the ten minute warning was announced, so I quickened my step.

When I returned, Remy was stroking the neck of my gelding and speaking to him in a low soothing voice. "All set?" he asked when I got close enough.

"I think so." I untied Raven and swung onto his back.

"How about your riding partner?"

I tightened the strap on my helmet. "I hope so."

He chuckled. "Me, too."

Scott trotted past as I reined Raven's head around, and we rode toward the gate together.

"Now, when we get up there, don't crowd the gate. Stay far enough back so riders can easily come and go."

"Five minutes," the head timer called.

We stopped at the large, plastic water troughs and allowed the horses one last chance to have a drink. Other riders were poised in groups here and there, waiting. As the horses drank their fill, I adjusted my seat and regathered the reins in my left hand. Scott seemed a little anxious as he pulled that disgusting cowboy hat farther down over his eyes.

"Oh, and when the gate opens," I began, "you don't have to ..."

Finally, the much-awaited announcement came. "The gate is now open."

"Is that it?" Scott asked, looking at me. "We're starting?"

"Yes, but as I was saying, you don't have to ..." But before I could finish, Scott prodded Raz into a lope and cut off two older female riders who had been moving toward the gate.

"Damn hot shoe!" one of them called after him.

"Must be another rodeo clown," the other one said.

"I'll say. Did you get a look at that hat he was wearing?" Then they both laughed as their horses trotted through the gate, pausing just long enough to call out their numbers before heading out onto the trail.

"Oh, you have no idea," I muttered as Raven and I did the same.

Chapter 25

The first 30 minutes of the ride we traveled up a gentle climb and onto a plateau, and there seemed to be an endless line of riders in front of and behind me, some passing and others being passed. But as we crossed the flat piece of land, each horse and rider found their pace, and we began to spread ourselves out until, at last, I found myself alone on the trail as it moved to the left and along the edge of the drop-off. Not completely alone, of course, because I could still hear the conversations of those riders who chose to stay together, and I could see in the distance in both directions helmeted heads as they bobbed along on their merry way. Even so, I was sufficiently isolated and lost myself in Raven's rhythm, feeling his massive body moving beneath me, our breathing synchronized.

The trail moved away from the edge and climbed toward the nearest peak. I shifted my weight forward slightly, and we easily reached the top. Lingering briefly, I marveled at the bare, wrinkled slopes of the surrounding mountain ranges, framing the deep blue sky, as well as the undulating landscape that hid the small neighboring communities that I knew were there.

We left the vantage point and dropped onto another large, gently sloping plateau. Moving at a competitive gait, we crossed it in less than half of an hour. The trail then steepened considerably and meandered downward through a ravine. I could see where it eventually connected with a more established road, so I pulled out my map and determined my location as well as the location of the water supply. We were making good time.

As I put my map away, I noticed two small groups of riders behind us just starting to cross the plateau. "Time to get moving," I told Raven. "But I think I'll take advantage of the downhill and stretch my legs a bit." I dismounted, and we began our descent.

Jogging alongside my horse, I wondered how Scott and Raz were doing. Hopefully, he'd slowed down some and wasn't pushing his horse too hard. *Time will tell.*

When we reached the bottom, I was glad to see the road was sand rather than gravel. "Okay Raven, now we can have some fun." I climbed back on and nudged the gelding into a canter. As we flew along, I was certain my horse was grinning as much as I was. By the time we reached the water troughs, we both were breathing hard, and he'd worked up a nice sweat.

I walked him around for a few minutes before letting him drink, and we shared a snack of apples, carrots, and horse cookies. They weren't bad, but I had to agree with Scott; they were rather dry, and I was glad we both had lots of water to wash them down.

Our brief rest over, we turned right and picked up the trail on another narrow jeep track, and immediately began a very steep climb. Transferring my weight to the stirrups, I leaned over the saddle until my body was almost parallel with Raven's neck. He lowered his head as he dug in, and we charged up the hill. Near the top, the trail turned to the left and leveled out. I slowed him to a walk, his head bobbing up and down with each long stride.

The trail continued just below the ridge top, weaving around large outcroppings of rock. It was definitely hotter than when we started, so I kept him at a walk, giving him plenty of time to recover. Eventually we made another turn to the right onto the eastern edge of a plateau we'd crossed earlier. Raven again hit his pacer-like stride, and we headed for the next peak.

As we circled around it, I detected movement below us and spotted a small herd of wild horses. Several of them stopped grazing and raised their heads to watch us pass. My body tensed with apprehension, but my horse didn't seem to notice. Relieved, I was just relaxing back into the rhythm of the ride when the trail made a sharp turn to the left and dropped down onto the flat and the road leading back to base camp.

Several riders were in front of us, and the moment we reached the road, Raven broke into a canter without being prompted. "You're more competitive than I am, aren't you Big Fella," I said, patting his sweat-soaked neck.

In no time at all, we caught up to the first group of three. "Passing on the left," I called as we went by, and all three waved an acknowledgment. This repeated each time I passed other groups or single riders, some of them already out of the saddle and jogging alongside their animals.

Wondering if I'd somehow missed the place where the trail had first left the main road, I was shocked to suddenly see base camp only a few hundred yards away.

Dammit! I reined Raven in, bailed off, and began leading him at a slow trot for a few minutes before dropping back to a walk.

Ignoring the cheers and applause as I passed through the gate, I called out my number and went straight to the pulse area.

"Too high," the woman with a stethoscope said. "Do what you need to do to get it down."

Stupid! Stupid! Stupid! I led Raven to the nearby watering tanks, and while he got a drink, I pulled the sponge out of my saddlebags and stuck it in the water. When it was saturated, I squeezed it over his head and neck. I repeated this a couple more times, and then I walked him over to the trailer.

Raz, still wearing his saddle, was inside the small corral, munching on some hay. Scott was sitting on the Dooley's tailgate and feeding his own face.

"Hey, Sarah. About time you showed up."

"Funny, Scott. Real funny." I tied Raven's lead rope to the side of the trailer and began pulling off tack. "How long did it take you to ride the loop?"

Scott shoved the last of his sandwich into his mouth and hopped off the tailgate. "Just over an hour; maybe an hour fifteen."

Shaking my head, I grabbed the sponge again and this time squeezed water onto Raven's back and rump.

"What are you doing that for?"

"I need to bring Raven's pulse rate down before I can take him over to the vet to be checked out."

"Oh man, I could've used that. Took almost the full thirty minutes to get Raz's to slow down."

I untied the lead rope. "If you'd taken off his saddle, that would've helped."

"Why didn't you tell me about all this?"

"Because I thought we'd be riding together and was planning on sharing all this along the way. Where's Remy?"

"Don't know. After he dug me out some leftover salad and beans, he and the four-legged duo took off. Speaking of which, the sandwiches they put out are pretty good." He pointed toward where we'd had the rider meeting the evening before. "Want me to go get something for you?" He paused. "But you're on your own if you want something outta the ice chest. Remy gave me strict orders to stay out of it. Don't know why, though."

Oh, I do! "No thanks, I'll grab something later." I started toward the pulse check area but stopped and turned around. "Did you give your horse some oats?" I asked as I dug my rider card out of the saddlebags.

"No."

"Well, you need to."

"Aye aye, captain," Scott said, giving me a cursory salute.

Oh brother! "Come on Raven, let's go see how you're doing." I was halfway across camp when I ran into Remy.

"There you are. I've been watching for you ever since Scott came back. How'd your ride go?"

"Fine until the end," I replied and motioned for him to walk with me. "I did a really stupid thing."

"Oh?"

"I missed the place where I'd plan to dismount and walk in with Raven, so his pulse didn't come down like it should have when we got back. I've been doing what I can to lower it, but that means I'll be in the hold longer than I'd hoped."

He stopped and turned to face me. "It won't keep you out of the race will it?"

I shook my head. "I don't think so. It was just an amateurish thing to do."

He patted me on the arm and said, "Go on then, and I'll have something for you to eat when you get back."

We parted company, and I stood in line for the woman with the stethoscope. When it was my turn, she listened for a full minute, shook her head and then frowned. "Hang on, let me do that again." She reapplied her stethoscope behind Raven's front left leg. "You're fine," she said and jotted down the time on my rider card.

Feeling slightly better, I led Raven directly to the vet check area and anxiously waited while the control judge completed her exam. Finally, she said the three words I'd been hoping to hear. "Fit to continue."

"Thanks," I said, and Raven and I headed back to the trailer for some rest and something to eat.

Chapter 26

Watching the large red numbers of the timer's clock slowly change was pure agony. Scott, as well as several other riders, had left nearly half an hour earlier, but my hold time wasn't up yet.

While I waited, I studied the map for the second loop of the 30-mile ride, which resembled a lopsided eight tipped to one side. I again located the placement of the water troughs and determined the best place to dismount at the end of the ride and walk in. Feeling prepared and trying to kill time, I guided Raven over for one last drink. When I returned to the head timer's table, the red numbers I'd been waiting for were displayed on the clock. I called out my number as I passed through the gate, and we headed out at an easy trot.

This time we stayed to the right and traveled along a very narrow jeep track until it connected with a wider road. At that point, the blue ribbons marking the trail indicated a sharp turn to the left onto a single-track headed north.

Raven lengthened his stride, and we easily traversed the gentle slope. Just as we reached the top, I spotted a rider leading a horse and walking the wrong direction. A little closer and I instantly recognized the sleeveless western shirt. Urging my horse into a lope, we covered the remaining distance in less than a minute.

"What happened?" I asked Scott when I pulled Raven up next to him.

"Damn snake!" he replied. "We were traveling along just fine when this huge rattler shoots across the trail, sending Spaz here into a tizzy and dumping me on my ass."

"Looks like you landed on the other end," I said, nodding at the tacky-looking blood along the hairline of his sweaty forehead. "Guess your hat didn't help much." I dismounted and stepped over to get a closer look.

"Well, actually it did." He gingerly touched the wound. "After his initial reaction, Raz started trying to stomp the snake. I didn't want him to get bit, so I threw my hat at it, trying to scare it off."

"Did it work?"

"Yeah, except then the stupid horse stomped my hat." He reached into his backpack, which was hanging from the horn of the saddle and held it out. The crown had been completely crushed and most of the brim was torn loose.

"But I saw him limping. Did the snake bite him?"

"Not that I could see." Scott stuffed the hat back into his backpack and lifted Raz's left front hoof. "He's got a rock wedged in under his shoe, and I can't budge it."

"Did you try a hoof pick?"

"Of course I did, but it's jammed in between his frog and the shoe. I think I'm gonna have to pull the shoe off in order the get the rock out. The thing I'm worried about is having Raz walk on it much further. We've already come quite a ways."

"I agree. Didn't anyone else stop to help?"

"No. I didn't realize I had a problem for a while. We were just taking it slow, trying to recoup. A few riders passed us; then when I was checking his hoof, a couple of old ladies rode by, and one of them hollered something about his shoe."

I immediately knew who he was talking about and turned my head, so he wouldn't see the grin I knew would be emerging.

"I hollered back that it was a rock not the shoe, but they just kept going."

"Okay," I said when I could speak without laughing. "We need to figure out how to get you two back to camp." But I wasn't sure how. It had to be getting close to a hundred degrees, and it would be about an hour, if not longer, before the drag riders made their sweep. I had a hoof boot in my saddlebags but finishing the ride without it would be like driving a car without a spare, and I wasn't even certain it would prevent permanent damage to Raz's hoof if Scott tried to walk him all the way back. I didn't have my cell phone and had no idea who I'd call if I did. I'd crossed a jeep track about fifty yards back, so someone should be able to get fairly close with a trailer.

I was just about to suggest that I ride back for help when I spotted a large dust cloud to the southeast. *It has to be a vehicle.* "I have an idea," I told Scott as I scrambled back into the saddle. "Give me your map."

He reached into the side pocket of his backpack and pulled out his rider card smeared with what I hoped was maple oatmeal muffin. "Hang on, it's around here somewhere." As he searched, the dust cloud continued its approach.

Next he looked in the main compartment of the backpack but came up empty. Searching through his clothing, he finally found the map in a pocket of his western shirt.

"Be right back," I said as I snatched it out of his hand. I swung Raven around and rode cross-country on an intercept course. Grateful it was the beginning of the second loop, I knew I could push Raven a little harder; however, there was no need. He seemed to sense the urgency of our side trip as he traveled at near breakneck speed. I let him navigate his own path through the sagebrush, with only minor adjustments being made to keep him on course. *Oh this is going to be close!*

As we dropped into a large depression in the landscape, I lost sight of the dust cloud. Riding up the other side, we burst over the top of a small ridge and dropped down onto the road about fifty yards in front of a Chevy flatbed pickup. The driver slammed on the brakes and slid to a stop. His door flew open, and he jumped out.

"What the hell are you doing?" the man yelled as he whipped the ball cap off of his head and rushed toward me.

"So sorry," I said, "but I need some help. My friend and I are riding in an endurance competition, and his horse has come up lame."

"Yeah, I know about the competition." He motioned toward his truck where a huge tank was strapped to the flatbed and had a three-inch hose attached to it. "I'm the one keeping the water troughs filled."

"Great. Do you have a pen?"

The man stared at me for a moment, then pulled one from his front shirt pocket and handed it to me as I unfolded Scott's map.

"My friend is near this road." I drew an X on the map. "It's a fairly large flat area, so someone should be able to get a trailer in there to pick them up."

He looked at the map. "Yeah, I'm pretty sure that would be doable. I'll let Margo know as soon as I get back."

"That would be perfect. Thanks so much," I said, handing him the map. "And again, I'm really sorry I scared you. I had no idea you were so close."

"Yeah, well ..." He tugged his hat back onto his head. "You need to be more careful." He returned to his truck, and Raven and I climbed back up the small ridge, pausing at the top just long enough to wave as he passed by.

When I got back to where Scott was waiting, I explained the plan. "Sounds good," he said. "I still have a couple bottles of water and a few snacks. I'll be fine until the trailer gets here."

"You don't want me to wait here with you?"

"What for? Help's on the way, and you have a ride to finish."

I really did want to finish but didn't feel like I should just take off and leave him. "That's okay. I don't mind."

"Oh cut the crap, Sarah. You know you want to keep going." The man could be so annoying, but he did know me.

"If you're sure you don't mind."

"Go on, get out of here before you're dead last." I guided Raven back onto the single-track. "Good luck," he called, and we took off.

The trail took us northeast across another huge expanse. We'd lost quite a bit of time, but I didn't want to push Raven too hard after our impromptu side trip, so I kept him at a slower trot than usual. A half-hour later, we finally crossed another road and continued to follow the trail south.

Soon, I became aware of a small herd of antelope off to my left. Wondering what had stirred them up, I scanned the area behind them and spotted a group of people on horseback. Assuming they were the drag riders coming in off the first loop of the 50-mile ride, I didn't pay much attention. That is, until they merged onto my trail, also heading south. Curious about what was going on, I encouraged Raven to hasten his pace in hopes of catching up to them. The opportunity came soon afterward when we all arrived at the watering troughs.

Eight tub-like containers were lined up along the edge of a wide, dirt road. Some were still filled to the brim with clear water, and if they had been a little bit bigger, I'd have jumped into one.

Six other riders were gathered close by, including a young boy on a pony. "Hi there, how's your ride?" a man on an Appaloosa asked as we approached.

The four female riders I'd followed in exchanged glances, obviously sharing some kind of secret. "Better now," one of them replied as their horses moved in to drink.

Raven and I navigated to the other side of the troughs, and I chose one further down. "Did you have a problem?" I asked. "I observed you come in from the east and get back on the trail."

"Damn." This one was wearing a helmet camera. "I was hoping no one saw that."

"Take a wrong turn?"

"Quite the opposite, actually. We were so busy talking, none of us noticed that the trail turned to the right, so we just kept going until we realized we hadn't passed any ribbons for awhile. And now we're really behind."

"These things happen. Poor Toby here was having a hard time in this heat," the man said, pointing at the pony, "so we've been here longer than usual, letting him rest."

Finished drinking, Raven began nodding his head up and down and splashing water out of the container. Then he stomped his right front hoof into the mud puddle he'd made.

"What on earth are you doing?" I backed him up away from the container but as soon as I took the pressure off of the reins, he stepped forward and stomped in the puddle again. Finally, I understood what he wanted and dug the sponge out of the saddlebags. Dangling it by its cord, I dropped it into the closest trough and squeezed it over his head and neck, making sure to squeeze a little over myself as well.

"Looks like he has you well-trained," another rider from the group of four remarked.

"So it would seem." I traded the sponge for the plastic bag of food. "How about a snack?" The gelding curled his neck around and, using his nimble lips, took the pieces of apple and carrot I offered him as well as a few horse cookies. One more drink of water for each of us, and we were ready to go.

"Well, good luck to you," I said as I guided Raven past the two groups of riders, anxious to get ahead of them.

"Happy riding," the man on the Appaloosa called as he waved good-bye.

Chapter 27

About a hundred yards past the water troughs, the trail left the road and headed to the right on what resembled a wide single-track trail rather than a jeep track. Curving to the southwest, it veered toward the upper end of a small mountain range and headed into a tight canyon. Glancing over my shoulder, I could see the ten riders I'd left behind traveling in a long, single file line.

Determined to stay ahead of them, I signaled Raven to pick up his pace and we entered the canyon. The trail followed the narrow jeep track as it moved from one side of a dry creek bed to the other. As we climbed, the trail continued to narrow until we were confined to the creek bed, which was filled with large boulders and loose rock requiring tremendous concentration to navigate. We'd almost reached the top when a coyote suddenly darted out of an adjacent draw right in front of us. Startled, it took a few minutes to regain our pace and composure, but my upper body remained tense.

Still following the creek bed, the trail took us around the base of a rocky knoll decorated with some kind of white mineral and up a slight incline until it emptied onto the road where I'd flagged down the Chevy flatbed. Back on more solid footing, Raven broke into a canter and, thanks to the rocking motion of his massive body and the rhythmic sound of his hooves, I felt the tension flow out of my neck and shoulders.

A little more than an hour into the ride, I again passed the intersection I'd first encountered and began the second part of the figure eight. Dropping back to a quick trot, we followed another single-track to the left as it wound up the hillside and finally climbed up a steep incline to the ridge above.

Sensing that I was close to where I'd left Scott, I pulled out my map and verified my location and the spot where I planned to dismount and walk in. From my vantage point at the top of the hill, I could see the main road back to the camp far below me and decided to make one last push. I secured my map, shared a couple bottles of water with Raven, and took off.

We made good time down the gentle slope, passing two riders just before coming out on the main road. Again, Raven increased his speed on his own, and I actually had to check his pace a couple of times.

Sweat dripped from my face and ran down my back. Concerned about Raven, I reined him in to a trot and grabbed the last bottle of water out of the saddlebags. I took a quick sip then leaned forward and poured the rest over his head. "Doing great," I told him. "We're almost there."

A few minutes later, we reached the cool down spot I'd selected, and I jumped off. Leaving the reins over his neck, I loosened the lead rope from my saddle, and we continued at a slow jog. Not sure how long I could maintain that speed in the heat, I focused on the single rider ahead of us, hoping to pass him before I was forced to slow down.

Reminded of when Raven got away from me during the wild horse roundup, I watched my feet shoot out in front of me, one at a time, over and over. Slowly, the distance between us and the rider lessened until we were jogging side by side. My breathing became more difficult. *I have to slow down.* At that moment, we moved ahead; the other rider had dropped back to a walk. Determined to stay ahead, I set a goal and began counting.

Forty-eight ... forty-nine ... fifty. I decelerated to a brisk walk and lengthened my stride, Raven matching my pace. Deep inhales of air helped regulate my breathing and alleviate the stitch in my side. Passing the place where I'd dismounted last time, I again heard applause and cheering coming from the gate ahead and was confident that Raven's pulse are would be lower. I was right.

"Sixty," the woman with the stethoscope said. "You're good to report to the vet check area." As she recorded the time on my rider card, I checked out the line. All the vets were occupied and three more horses were waiting, so I had plenty of time to cool him down.

Back at the trailer, I pulled off Raven's saddle as well as my helmet. Both of us were drenched. After making sure I had my rider card, I snagged the sponge and led him back to the vet check area. A quick stop for a drink and a dousing, then we got in line.

I anxiously waited for my turn and tried not to be nervous. We'd had a great ride without any trip ups or tumbles, and I'd given him a good cool down. But there always could be issues a rider hadn't noticed; a pulled muscle, dehydration, internal problems.

As soon as one of the vets waved me over, I spotted Scott leading his horse from the first-aid station at the back of the vet check area. The wound on his head had been covered by a white bandage, and neither of them seemed to be limping. I handed over my rider card and waved to him.

He returned my wave and led Raz over closer. "Glad to see you made it back."

"I did. Only have to get through this last check, and we're done."

"Great. I'll hang out and we can walk back together."

I nodded and turned my attention back to Raven's assessment. Poked, prodded, listened to, and trotted out and back, he passed. Delighted beyond words, I turned in my rider card, and the four of us headed for the trailer.

"So what was the verdict on all the injuries?" I asked.

"Well, no stitches for me and a little packing and hoof tape for Raz." He stopped and pointed at the Arabian's feet. "Check it out; they say it's way better than duct tape."

"Huh," I said, looking at the piece of black material stuck to the left front hoof and resembling a cupcake wrapper. "I may need to get some of that."

We started for the trailer again, but there was a tug on my lead rope. I turned around just in time to see Raven collapse onto his front legs. My initial reaction was panic until he folded up his hind legs and lowered his rump to the ground. Then he flopped over and rolled from side to side, the whole time thrashing his head and moving his feet as if loping in midair. Finally, he

223

struggled to his feet and shook his whole body, creating a small cloud of dust.

Good grief! "Are you happy now, you silly horse?"

He nodded his massive head, and we continued on our way.

"Here you go," Remy said, handing me a glass of sweet tea with fresh ice cubes floating in it.

"Where'd the ice come from?" I asked after finishing it in four gulps. I dug out a cube and held it against the inside of my left wrist as well as my temples and enjoyed the instant cooling sensation.

"Told you. I've got my sources."

"What time do you wanna get outta here?" Scott asked, sipping on his own glass of the cold drink.

"I'd like Raven to get as much rest as possible before pulling out. How about right after the awards ceremony? That'll put us back to your place between eight-thirty and nine o'clock. Allow another half an hour to swap trailers, and we should be home by eleven at the latest."

"Works for me," Scott said.

"Great. I'm going to take a nap." I stepped toward the door of the trailer. "Wake me up in about an hour."

"You bet," Scott replied as he poured himself another glass of Remy's sweet tea.

The crowd's constant chatter grew in volume until Margo, the ride manager, stepped to the front and raised her hands. "I, again, want to thank everyone that particpated in our competition," she said when the conversations had ceased. "We had fifty-two riders in the 50 and thirty-eight riders in the 30. Overall, a great turnout, and we only had a few injuries this year. Mostly bumps and bruises. Oh, and one black eye but no broken bones."

"You still haven't told me how you did that," I said to Bernie over the sound of the clapping. Charlene and Louise looked eager to hear her response as well.

"It was no big deal," Bernie said. "Just before leaving the hold, I was checking the hoof boot on my horse's front foot, and she lifted her leg as I bent down and caught me right in the eye."

"You're lucky it wasn't your nose," Louise said. "Probably would've broken it."

Bernie smiled and nodded. "You're probably right."

"We've posted the top ten in each ride." Margo continued, gesturing toward a large piece of cardboard hanging on the fence. "And we have two awards for Best Condition I'd like to acknowledge. For the 50-mile, Louise Tykes has won it again, for the sixth year in a row."

The crowd applauded, and we all congratulated her as she left our group and went to collect her award.

"And for the 30-mile, Annette Harding." Amid another wave of applause, the older woman who had called Scott a "hot shoe" stepped forward. "Congratulations, ladies. Well done."

"For those of you heading home this evening, don't forget to have your proof of ownership and health certificate handy, especially if you're heading north on Highway 395. There's an agricultural inspection station just past the California border."

There's something I haven't thought about. "You've got Raz's paperwork, don't you?" I asked Scott.

"Sure. It's right there in the jockey ..." He stopped, his facial expression more serious than I'd ever seen. "Aw, shit. It's in the jockey box of *my* truck. So no, I don't have my horse's paperwork."

"Aw shit," I echoed. "So now what are we going to do?"

Louise, who had obviously been listening to our conversation, leaned across Bernie and curled her right index finger at me a couple times. "Don't sweat it," she whispered as I leaned closer. "When you drive out of here, turn right instead of left, and the road will take you back to the highway well past the border and the inspection station."

"Really?" A huge wave of relief washed over me. "That's great. Thanks."

"You're welcome. Most of us heading north go that way anyway."

"Problem solved," I said to Scott.

"Awesome. Now, whatd'ya say we get out of here?"

"I'm ready. Just want to check out the top ten and then I'll meet you at the trailer."

"Gotcha." Scott strutted off, and I joined several others looking at the posted list. I'd barely finished in the top ten, which sounded impressive until I reminded myself that at least a third of the riders had experienced worse delays of their own. Even so, I was proud of what Raven and I had accomplished and looked forward to the next time we could compete—just the two of us!

Chapter 28

"I'm really glad we decided to spend the night at Scott's," I said to Remy as we pulled onto Highway 299, heading east toward the center of town. The clearing of a traffic collision just north of Ravendale had delayed our trip home by almost an hour. "I could hardly keep my eyes open by the time we pulled in."

"I was a might tuckered out myself," Remy agreed.

I coasted to a stop at the convergence of the two main highways that pass through Alturas. "You know," I began, "besides spending time out on the trail with Raven, the next best thing about this weekend is I didn't think about Ida Dudley once."

"Well, now that there is a good thing," Remy replied. I had to agree, especially if I ended up dealing with her over the next two weeks.

I glanced at the fuel indicator. Having less than a quarter of a tank, I pulled into the gas station just across the intersection. As I was fueling, a black Volkswagen Jetta pulled in next to us, and a man wearing blue jeans, a dark green T-shirt and a Copenhagen ball cap climbed out. Paying no attention to anyone around him, he began filling the small car with gas.

"What brings you back to town, Nate?" I asked.

At the mention of his name, the man froze and then slowly turned to look at me. "Oh hello, Deputy," he said when he realized who I was. "Sorry, what did you say?"

"I asked what brings you back to town?"

"Just have some business to tend to."

I bet you do! "Working on another roundup?"

He readjusted his hat. "No. It's personal."

Before I could think of anything else to say, a loud banging drew my attention to a black Dodge Ram. Towing a silver livestock trailer, it had pulled up to the four-way stop.

"That your horse making all that ruckus?" Nate asked.

"No, I think it's coming from over there." I pointed at the rig. "Must be hauling something that doesn't like being in a trailer." But as I looked again, it appeared to be empty.

Nate turned to see what I was looking at. "Sonofabitch! He's got her again!" He shut off the pump and jerked the nozzle out of his tank.

"Who?" I asked. "And what do you mean again?"

Nate hesitated for just a moment. "That's Coop," he said, pointing at the vehicle as it completed the turn and headed south on Main Street, "and it sounds like he's got that damn protestor in his trailer."

"You mean *he's* the one who kidnapped Ida?"

Nate pulled a twenty-dollar bill out of his pocket and stuck it through the handle of the gas pump. Then he dashed around his car and climbed in behind the wheel. Without hesitating, I jumped into the passenger seat.

"Let's go," I said, fastening my seatbelt.

"What are you doing?" Nate demanded.

"Apprehending a kidnapper. Now, step on it!"

He fired the engine and stomped on the accelerator, shifting into second gear before we reached the street. Tires screeched as he pulled into traffic, scarcely missing two cars. I began to have serious doubts about my decision but kept my concerns to myself lest I distract him.

Thanks to light Sunday morning traffic, Nate easily caught up to the truck and trailer, but by the time we passed the park, we were traveling about 60 miles per hour. As we rocketed up and across the overpass, I dug out my phone and called for help.

"Sheriff's Office."

"Ira, it's Sarah."

He let out a huge sigh and said, "What do you want now? Need another helicopter?"

"No, but we need backup."

"We? Backup?"

I quickly explained what was happening, gave our location and the direction we were heading. "We've got to stop this guy before someone gets hurt." We flew by the wildlife refuge.

"Understood. I'll dispatch a couple of our deputies and see if I can get some help from the highway patrol."

"That'll be perfect. Just make sure they all know about the woman in the back of the trailer. We don't need any risky maneuvers trying to stop him."

"Got it."

"Oh, and Ira?"

"Yes."

"There's an old guy sitting in my white Dooley at the gas station across the street. Go tell him I'll be back as soon as I can."

"Seriously?"

"Oh come on, Ira. Please."

"Fine." He disconnected as the Jetta sailed across the South Fork of the Pitt River.

"You got a gun?" I asked Nate, tucking my phone back into my pocket.

He glanced at me. "No."

Just my luck to hook up with a cowboy that doesn't carry a gun. "Does ... what did you say his name is?"

"Coop."

"Coop," I repeated. "Does Coop have a gun?"

Another quick glance. "No ... maybe." He paused, and I saw his fingers tighten on the steering wheel. "Hell, I don't know."

Oh great! "Listen, we're on a long straightaway, and if we can get ahead of Coop, maybe we can slow him down a little. Can you see if there are any cars coming?"

Nate tipped his head to the left and maneuvered the car across the center line but swerved back in behind the trailer, just before a Swift Transportation semitruck zipped by. He tried again and, this time, managed to pull into the northbound lane. Slowly, we gained on the Dodge Ram until we were traveling side by side. The driver glanced over at us and then did a double take. Before I could motion for him to pull over, he leaned forward slightly and increased his speed.

"Keep going," I shouted at Nate. "We've got to get ahead of him."

"I'm trying! We're practically doing 80 now!"

"Hurry up! We're going to run out of straightaway." The small car edged ahead for a brief moment until the truck increased its speed again. Back and forth, back and forth, each vehicle in turn pulling ahead of the the other until the car's front end began to shudder.

"Holy crap!" Nate exclaimed, looking at the speedometer. "We've hit a hundred miles an hour!"

"Car! Car! Car!" I screamed. I threw my hands against the dashboard and braced myself.

The wrangler slammed on the brakes and, as soon as the back end of the trailer passed us, swerved into the right-hand lane, barely missing the oncoming car. "Omigod, that was close!"

"Pull over," I commanded. "Pull over right now!" *What was I thinking!* So focused on catching Ida's kidnapper, I didn't consider the consequences of my actions. "I think we should turn around and head back."

"And let him get away?" he asked, easing onto the shoulder and coming to a complete stop.

"I've called it in, and one of ..." My phone rang. With trembling fingers, I dug it out of my pocket.

"Hello?"

"They're in the process of setting up a roadblock." It was Ira.

"Where?"

"Right at the end of the passing lanes, just north of Likely."

"How'd they get there so fast?"

"A CHP officer happened to be at a pancake breakfast at the Likely Volunteer Fire Department, so they're helping get some equipment and barricades in place."

"Thanks." I snapped my phone shut. "They're going to try and stop him at Likely," I told Nate. "Let's go!"

"Now we're talking." He threw the transmission into first gear, and we took off. Without us in pursuit, I hoped Coop had reduced his speed, making his encounter with the roadblock less dangerous.

We caught up to him a few minutes later. "Hang back," I told Nate. "No sense making him nervous." I glanced at the speedometer and was relieved to see that Coop had dropped back to the speed limit.

Moments later, he reached the double passing lanes. "Here we go. The roadblock should be at the bottom of this hill." Seconds ticked by until the taillights of the trailer suddenly came on. It fishtailed a couple of times before it and the truck flew off the road to the right, creating an explosion of dirt and grass. Surprisingly, both remained upright.

Nate slid to a stop where the rig had left the roadway, and we bailed out.

"Detain that man," I called to the the highway patrolman who was running toward the truck with his gun drawn. Hurrying as fast as I could, I headed for the back of the trailer. "Hang on, we're coming!" With Nate's help, I unlatched the door and threw it open.

Ida Dudley lay on the floor, her hands and feet tied together behind her back, and duct tape covered her mouth. I tried to untie the rope, but her struggling had tightened the knots.

"Here," Nate said, handing me a knife he'd pulled out of the three-inch sheath that hung from his belt. "Use this."

I cut Ida free and then very carefully pulled the tape away from her face. "Are you okay? Are you hurt anywhere?"

She shook her head. "I'm fine," she panted. "How did you know I was in here?"

"We heard you pounding the side of the trailer," I said as I led her outside. "And Nate here, recognized the driver."

"I'm sure he did," Ida sneered, brushing herself off and trying to smooth her tangled mane of hair.

"What's that supposed to mean?" Nate demanded.

"It means I saw that man's face this time, and I know he's one of *your* wranglers."

"Now, hang on there. He isn't on the payroll anymore and wasn't even supposed to be here," Nate said.

"Well, that didn't stop him from grabbing me, did it?" Ida countered.

"So is this the same guy that grabbed you before?" I asked.

"It certainly is," Ida replied. "I recognized the voice right away. And now that I've seen who it is, I'm not one bit surprised."

"Anyone need medical attention?" a man asked as he approached, carrying a large medic bag.

"Maybe you should go with him," I suggested to Ida, welcoming the interruption. "Just to make sure you're all right." Without another word, she followed the EMT back to a fire truck parked nearby.

"Do you know what she's talking about?" I asked Nate. He nodded.

"Well?"

"You better ask him," he said, gesturing toward his friend.

"Fine. I will."

I walked over to the driver who had been handcuffed and was sitting on the ground near his truck. As I got closer, I felt a twinge of familiarity that I couldn't quite put my finger on. "You want to tell me why you had a woman tied up in your trailer?"

"I ain't got nothing to say," the man replied in one of the deepest voices I'd ever heard. *Chocolaty?*

"Aw come on, Coop."

"And I told you to butt the hell out," he snarled at Nate. "I did what I had to do. That loudmouthed bitch got me fired!"

I was about to try a different approach when a vehicle from the Modoc County Sheriff's Office arrived and nosed in behind the fire truck. "I need to talk to that deputy," I said to Nate, "so, why don't you wait for me over by your car."

"Yeah, sure. Okay." He trudged over to his vehicle and leaned against the front right fender, his arms folded across his chest.

"Don't go anywhere," I said to Coop before strolling over to the deputy. "Hi, Joe. Good to see you."

"Hey, Sarah. So what do we have going on here?"

I briefly summarized the situation. "Looks to me like two counts of kidnapping and one count of reckless endangerment."

"Sounds about right," Joe agreed.

"And then, if you wouldn't mind taking the victim's statement, she's getting checked out by the EMT."

"Got it." Joe opened the back passenger door of his Chevy four-door pickup and went to collect the suspect. I headed the other direction.

"It appears I won't be getting any information out of Coop, so maybe you ought to fill me in on what happened," I said, leaning on the fender next to Nate.

"I don't want to get him in trouble."

"Nate, he's already in trouble, and you might be, too if you don't help me. Did you know he was going to kidnap Ida?"

"Oh, hell no. Like I said, he wasn't even supposed to be in the area. That's why I was surprised when I spotted him up on the hillside the day of the roundup."

"Did you see him again after that?"

He shook his head. "No, but the morning we left Cedarville, I took a chance and stopped by the hotel to see if he was there."

"Was he?"

"Yeah, but there was no answer when I knocked on his door." He shook his head again. "I hollered at him through the door not to do anything stupid."

"But by then it was already too late," I added.

"Yeah." Nate paused for a while and watched as Joe loaded his friend into the patrol unit. "I'd hoped he'd just go on home, but when I couldn't get ahold of him for a whole week, I figured I'd better come see if he was still around and what he was up to."

"When was that?"

"Friday. He wasn't at the hotel any more, so I drove around for a while and found his trailer parked behind the fairgrounds. That told me he was still there somewhere, but I didn't see any sign of his horse."

"Don't you mean *your* horse?" I asked.

"Used to be, but I gave him to Coop a couple years ago. Wait ... how did you know that?"

"Well, it was found mixed in with a small herd on a local ranch and, after checking out who'd adopted it, I was certain you were somehow behind all this but didn't have any solid evidence."

He straightened. "Me? I could never ..."

"Do you remember what you said at the roundup after Ida got there?" He slowly turned his head from side to side. "Something about what should be done with her?"

Again, he began to shake his head but stopped, and his eyes widened. "Oh ... yeah." He slumped against his car again.

"But even before that discovery, the fact that your truck and livestock trailer matched the description of those suspected in her kidnapping, I thought I'd figured out who'd grabbed her. But when I played a recording of your voice ..."

"*My* voice?"

I nodded. "A recording made during your crew's interviews."

"Oh, yeah."

"Anyway, she claimed none of the wranglers sounded like the guy who'd grabbed her—another dead end. But, when I saw you today, my suspicions returned," I said, shaking my head. "So, when did you find Coop?"

"Well, after searching all day, I'd stopped to grab a bite to eat and saw the article in the paper about the kidnapped protestor being found and that she was in a hospital in Alturas. That's when I had a pretty good idea where to find him, so I got a room for the night and headed over the mountain the next day."

"That would've been yesterday?"

"Yeah. On the way into town, I saw his truck parked at a motel on the outskirts, so I pulled in and waited. When he came out of his room, I confronted him. Of course, he denied having anything to do with her and drove away. I followed him for the rest of the day, but nothing happened.

"When I got up this morning, he was gone. I looked around for him for a little while and, when I couldn't find him, decided to go home. That's when I ran into you."

"Yeah," I said as I watched the members of the Likely Volunteer Fire Department load the last of the barricades into the bed of an older Ford pickup. The EMT had finished his examination of Ida, and she was giving her statement to Joe. In between her wild arm gestures, he'd look up from his notebook and glare in my direction. "Oh, this is gonna cost me," I murmured.

"What?" Nate asked.

"Nothing. Be right back." Finished, Joe was heading in my direction, and I went to meet him.

"Well, that was quite an experience," he said, "but I'm sure you already knew it would be."

"Yeah, sorry about that, but I thought it would be better if someone other than me talk to her."

"Well, if there's nothing else, I'll take my passenger back to the SO."

"Actually there is." I smiled my best smile, but I didn't think it was working.

"And that would be ..." He freed his sunglasses from his uniform shirt where he'd hung them during his visit with Ida and, using both hands, placed them back on his face.

"I need you to take Ida back to town as well."

"And do what with her?"

"Drop her off at Stony Ridge Lodge. That's where she's staying."

"Why can't you send her with the CHP?"

I pointed behind him. "Because he just left."

Joe turned around just in time to watch the cruiser make a U-turn and head back to Likely. "Fine," he said. "But you are going to owe me big time."

Chapter 29

Packed into the small conference room like sardines, we waited for Undersheriff Sandusky to begin. Anxious to share what he'd learned during the International Association of Chiefs of Police Conference and Exposition, he'd called an impromptu staff meeting. Only the knowledge that Sheriff Atkins would be there compelled most, if not all, of us to attend.

"I foresee big changes for this office," Sandusky began. "We'll have fully adjustable body armor that can hold additional armor plates, if necessary, and has the means of attaching a wide variety of gear and accessories."

Standing at the back of the room, I had an unobstructed view of everyone, including their subtle sidelong glances—and there were several of them.

"There's also a new line of tactical gear from riot helmets to shin guards, including shields and gas masks."

More glances and I'm fairly certain I detected a faint snicker or two.

The undersheriff went on about the latest forensic and investigative practices as well as the necessary equipment. "And ..." he said, turning to Sheriff Atkins, "I found the sessions on administration and training most informative, and I have some ideas on how to whip these deputies into shape."

Side conversations erupted all over the room, and I half-expected a chant of "Dirk the Jerk" to commence.

"Okay, thank you Sandusky," the sheriff said, getting to his feet. "And thank you all for coming in this morning. Have a good day and be safe."

"We all set?" Joe asked, stopping in front of me on his way out.

"Yeah, all set." I replied. I started to follow him, but curiosity got the better of me, so I lingered for a moment, feigning to retie the laces on one of my boots.

"Dirk," the sheriff said barely above a whisper, clearly having a difficult time maintaining his composure. "Did any of those session you attended teach anything about budgets or spending limitations?"

Sandusky frowned. "No."

"Then come into my office and let me *enlighten* you."

As I followed the sheriff out of the small conference room, I glanced back and momentarily locked eyes with the undersheriff. His face transformed from anger through rage to loathing, accentuated by his crimson complexion. I quickly continued my evacuation of the premises before he saw the involuntary smile blooming across my face. Feeling a strange sense of satisfaction, I rounded the corner, waved at Cindy as I passed her desk, and headed for the door.

"Sarah, hang on a second," she called. "There's a phone call for you." She held the receiver over the tall counter that surrounded her desk.

"Who is it?" I asked as I took it from her.

"Didn't get that far. The call came in just as you walked by."

Holding the receiver to my ear I said, "This is Deputy Murdock."

"Hi Deputy, it's Lulu DeLoure."

I made a face at Cindy. "Oh hello, Miss DeLoure." Cindy rolled her eyes back at me.

"Please call me Lulu. You're never going to guess what happened today."

"Oh? What?"

"Well ..."

Remy and I pulled up at the same time. "Glad you agreed to meet me," I said, opening the door of the Wagon Wheel Café.

"Thanks for the invite."

Without discussion, we moved forward toward the counter and I waved at Sal as we swung into our seats. "It's the least I can do after leaving you somewhat stranded for most of the day yesterday." I grabbed two menus from the holder and handed one to Remy.

"Yes, that was a might inconsiderate to go running off without so much as a how-do-you-do."

"I know, and I'm really sorry."

"What'll you two have?" Sal asked, posed with pen and pad ready to take our order.

"I believe I'll have me one of Cookie's club sandwiches and give me some of them home fries."

"Hmm, that sounds good," I said. "Make it two."

"Coming right up. Anything to drink?"

"Coffee for me," Remy said.

"And I'll have a Diet Pepsi."

"Got it." Sal made a final notation on our ticket before handing it off to the cook.

"Did you get any more information from that Coop fella as to why he grabbed that woman in the first place?" Remy asked after Sal set our drinks on the counter in front of us.

"Nelmer Cooper."

"How's that?"

"That's his real name. Nelmer Cooper."

"I can see why he'd go by Coop."

I nodded. "Me, too. Anyway, Ida had shown up at a roundup somewhere in Utah and was so disruptive that she and Coop had a screaming match, which ended when he shoved her to the ground."

"Hells bells. Did she press charges? Is that why he did it?"

"No, but she threatened to sue the government contractor if he wasn't fired." I took a long sip of my soda. "According to Nate, Coop has quite a temper, so he was determined to get revenge."

"I see. And what about Ida?"

"Oh, I'm fairly certain she'll be moving on in a day or so," I said and left it at that.

"Good deal." Remy slid his cup of coffee to one side just as Sal spun around from the pass-through, holding two large plates piled high with wedges of toasted sandwich and golden brown fries.

As I backed away from the restaurant, I noticed an unfamiliar Toyota Tundra parked in front of the Silver Spur Saloon. I didn't pay much attention to the black motorcycle secured with tie-downs in the bed, but when I drove by and saw the Kentucky license plate, it hit me. *Pete!*

I flipped a U-turn, parked next to the dark brown truck and went inside. Pete was sitting at the bar, chatting with Shellie.

"Sarah!" he said, sliding off the barstool and coming toward me. He started to give me a hug but stopped. "Or is it Deputy?"

"That depends. Is there anyone else here?"

"Don't think so. Shellie?"

"Just us," she said. "Daily Dude hasn't been in for a few days."

"Daily Dude?" I asked.

"Yeah, you know, that guy you asked me about last week," Pete replied.

A bolt of realization hit my brain. "That's why he looked familiar," I blurted.

"What are you talking about?"

"Come on," I said, leading him back toward the bar, "and I'll fill you in."

After making ourselves comfortable, I told Pete and Shellie about running into Nate and the high speed chase, which led to the inevitable capture of the kidnapper, as well as his vehement hostility toward Ida.

Shellie began nodding her head. "That would make sense. The few times I saw him, it was hard to get a read on him, you know. His aura was so close to his body, but it definitely was kind of a shadowy reddish color."

"And that means ..." I wasn't entirely sold on the whole aura thing, but past experience with Shellie led me to keep an open mind.

"Deep-seated anger," she said.

"That certainly fits."

"And so that guy—the guy who was coming in here for almost two weeks was the kidnapper?" Pete asked.

I nodded.

"Holy crap!"

I nodded again.

"And how about Ida?"

"Ugh!"

"What?"

"Well, someone saw Lulu's articles ..."

Pete interrupted. "What articles?"

"Tell you about those in a minute," I said. "Anyway, this person called and wants her to help make a documentary film for YouTube about Ida and her courageous fight to save wild horses."

"A documentary?"

"Yes, but don't tell Remy."

"Why not?" Shellie asked.

"Because, he and Lulu don't exactly get along."

Pete frowned.

"Remember the alpaca fiasco?"

"Oh yeah," he said. "No problemo."

"My lips are sealed," Shellie added.

"Good." I turned to Pete. "How was the anniversary party?"

"This is where I came in, as they say, so if you'll excuse me, I have some things to do in the back." Without waiting for a response, Shellie moved down the bar and disappeared through the door, leaving behind only a faint hint of patchouli.

"It was fine. My sister hosted the party, and lots of my folks' old friends came."

"So you had a good time?"

Pete didn't answer right away. "Yeah, I guess I did," he said, finally. "The best part was no one hassled me about my life choices."

I chuckled. "That's always a plus," I said, remembering my own experience when I decided to leave the FBI and move back to California to become a deputy. "And the truck?"

"Isn't it great? My sister had just upgraded to a fancier one to haul her horses around, and when I was telling her about needing someone to haul my bike trailer, she gave me her old one. I know," he said suddenly, a big grin on his face, "we should go for a ride this weekend."

"That sounds wonderful." I paused. "But I can't."

Pete's smile faded. "What do you mean you can't?"

"Remember that other deputy I mentioned that showed up to help with the kidnapper?"

"Yes," Pete said slowly.

"Well, he did something for me, and now I have to do something for him."

"What do you mean he did something for you?" His voice seemed a bit higher.

"Relax," I said, playfully elbowing him in the ribs. "I kind of delegated him to deal with Ida. In turn, he declared I owed him big time, so I have to take his patrol this weekend."

"But you hate working weekends."

"Yes, I do." *But it was so worth it!*